Kepler's Thorn

Curt Hampton

ISBN: 9798614704148

CONTENTS

ACKNOWLEDGMENTS

I doubt writing this book would have happened without the encouragement of my mentor, Andy. Thank you for your curiosity about the story idea I first described as "some astrophysics and some ridiculous physics" and for your initial thoughts on the first draft.
I also have to thank the people who read early drafts and contributed their feedback.

TO THE KIND READER

I sincerely apologize for the glut of chapters in this story.
It just happened.

PROLOGUE

I love scuba diving. Cave diving even more. In fact, that's where I am right now. I'm underwater, in a cave, in the dark, with only the clicking of my respirator, hissing of air through the hoses, and bubbling of exhaled air rising past the side of my head and up to the cave ceiling to keep me company. The squeezing pressure of my wetsuit and Buoyancy Control Device (BCD) vest make me feel calm and relaxed. Occasionally I catch myself softly humming. Humming is a subconscious thing I do. It also calms me, although I've never understood why.

Despite a feeling of solitude, I'm not alone. My dive partner, Reggie, is with me. I think he comes along mostly because he knows I need a buddy to do this. I can see the flash of his flashlight from behind me, so I know he's there. When we dive, we're never very far apart. You can't separate while diving, especially in a cave. When you're in a cave, you can't just go straight up to the surface if you get into trouble, so you have to stay with your buddy.

There are fish here with us. They're cave fish, blind and pale and pinkish. They usually stay still or glide slowly along the bottom. If anything surprises them, they bolt away with a quick flick of a pink tail. Even though the cave has plenty of room over our heads and is wide enough for Reggie and me to move comfortably, I've always wondered how the fish keep from running into a wall when they dart away.

The darkness is all encompassing and relaxing, but an odd feeling starts gnawing at the back of my mind. It's dark, but too dark. I hadn't noticed that I don't see Reggie's light sweeping back and forth anymore. I turn around to try to see him, but he isn't anywhere within as far as the beam of my flashlight goes. That's bad. I know I need to find him and find out if he's in trouble so I switch off my light to see if I can see any sign of his. There's a faint glow in the distance so I start moving that way.

As I go, I keep one hand in front of me so I don't run into anything big and click my light on for little bits to help with navigation and to let him see me if he's looking for me, too. Every time I do, though, it takes a little while for my eyes to adjust to the dark after turning it off again. I know that's slowing me down, but I want the light to go to him if he's looking. When I get closer to the glow, I can see it's him, but he isn't moving. He's unconscious and has been drifting away on the small current in the cave.

After reaching him, I grab his air gauge and see his air is out. He should have been checking that and let me know if he was low. We carry an extra safety air bottle with us, but his is nowhere in sight. In his condition, he isn't going to be able to use the safety bottle I have. I know it's going to take too long to get him out of the cave so we can surface for air, and the only thing I can think of is to start using my emergency air tank and try switching out his regular tank for mine. It has more pressure, and I hope it's enough to get him through the trip out.

I take out my regulator and start breathing with my emergency bottle. Then I start the process of taking off my BCD to get to my tank connections so I can put it on his. I do a barrel roll to get out of the shoulder straps, undo the tank straps, and start unscrewing it from the hose connector. It feels like it's taking forever, but it actually isn't. I'm kicking up all kinds of sediment as I manipulate the whole contraption and keep myself from floating away from him. Some of my weights were in the BCD so my body starts trying to float as soon as I take off my BCD. When I finally get the tank off, I flip Reggie over, unscrew his tank, screw mine on, and pop his regulator to get air into it.

At this point, I can see with my light that he's turning a light shade of blue. I know I have to get him out of the cave. The water is very cloudy now and it's hard to see, but I hope he's breathing. With one hand holding onto Reggie, I grab my compass and hold it close to my mask so I can see it. I turn in the general direction of the exit and start to swim. There isn't much more I can do for Reggie at the moment. I just hope I get him out in time.

Once we start moving away, the water gets less murky. I can see about five feet in front of us, then ten feet. There are no fish anywhere; I spooked them away with all of the activity. After what feels like an eternity, I glimpse the glow of the cave mouth and adjust course to head straight toward it. My heart and lungs are protesting from the effort of swimming through a small space with a full-sized man in tow, and my head is throbbing from the mental strain I'm under. There's a lot of sediment being kicked up in our wake, but I don't care because that's behind us. I'm focused on what's in front.

As we get out of the cave and up to the surface, it dawns on me how dumb I just was. I switched a whole scuba tank for Reggie, but each set up has a second respirator exactly for situations like this. Giving him the second respirator would have saved the time I wasted thrashing around to get out of my gear and switching his tank for mine. Stupid, stupid, stupid. You have to be so careful under water, and you practice these things when you become certified. In the heat of the moment, though, in the dark, imagining the weight of the rock ceiling over our heads, it didn't even dawn on me. As I was working to change the tanks, I was vaguely conscious of the second air line as a tangle of air hoses slowly flopped around, but I had pushed them all aside to get to the one I wanted.

At this point, Reggie has a little better color as I get him to shore and out of the water. He's alive and breathing. I flag someone down to call 911. I'm already not looking forward to having to talk about this in the future, but that's a conversation for later. We both screwed up badly. In my head, I know Reggie will never dive again. He wasn't a huge fan to start. As for me, I know I'll keep doing it. I'll take more training classes, though. I never want something like this to happen again.

1
JOURNAL
My Journal

Welcome to my journal. How to begin? Today was a gorgeous mid-January day. The sky was clear and the sun was bright after a couple of inches of snow last night. I've never kept a journal before so I guess writing about the weather is as good a way to start as any, especially after the day I had at work.

My name is Eugene Trevor David. Since those can all be first names, people get confused and call me a lot of different things: Gene, David, Mr. Gene, and Mr. David, mostly. Sometimes I think my parents named me this way consciously as a cruel joke. That's a horrible thing to do to a defenseless baby. At least they didn't name me "Sue", I guess.

I'm writing this journal because I want to keep my own record of what's happened. Other people will write from their perspective, but I want to keep mine. If this journal survives, maybe some memory of me will survive, too.

We got some awful news at work today. Actually, "awful" doesn't even begin to describe it. Mentally, emotionally, it's almost too much to grasp. I need to think things out in my head and write them out on these pages as a way of coping. More on that later, though.

Before getting too far into the recent events, here's a little more information about myself. I'm 38 years old and have a wife, Jenny, and a son, Max. Max is ten years old and is a bundle of energy. They don't know that I'm starting this journal. I can't tell them about it yet. Honestly, I don't know if I ever will.

We live in the house I grew up in. My father grew up in this house, too. Kind of creepy, I know, but I'm glad we live here. I know every inch of the house, the yard, the elm tree in the corner of the back yard, and the bomb shelter that Grandpa put in. He was afraid we were near Russian missile targets during the Cold War and built it to stay safe from nuclear bombs. I don't think he fully grasped how devastating a nuclear bomb would be. The family may have been safe from a bomb blast inside the shelter, but the subsequent radioactive fallout would have killed everyone eventually.

Grandpa was a builder, so the shelter is a custom job. I don't know if he would have understood the term back when he was building it, but it's "pimped out", which is to say it's very elaborate. The shelter is way overbuilt. I mean, it's huge. It's airtight and has its own air supply that'll last days. Thinking about it now, maybe he did understand fallout and didn't want to breathe air filled with radioactive dust. Anyway, it has space for months of food storage. The shelves are empty now, though, because there's been no need for a bomb shelter for decades. It's completely buried in the back yard and is only accessible from within the basement of the house, and even that entrance is hidden behind shelves and an extra hidden door that looks just like the rest of the wall. Between you and me, I think Grandpa was paranoid and had more than a few trust issues with his neighbors.

I've been Director of Disaster Management at the Federal Emergency

Management Agency (FEMA) in Colorado for the past 5 years. Before that, I was a team manager, and before that, I was a management official. Although my team is based here, we travel all over to help with disasters and manage the recovery resources. When there's enough notice, we'll sometimes go in before the disasters to do some planning, and afterwards when there isn't.

During my time here we've dealt with wildfires, hurricanes, tornadoes, earthquakes, and pretty much everything else that comes up. We joke at work that we'd be ready for a tsunami of puppies if one showed up. It'd be the cutest disaster anyone had ever seen. In fact, I have one mocked up as the screen saver on my computer as a way to remind myself to expect the unexpected.

We're based in Colorado because it's quiet in terms of disasters compared to other locations and is a central location for travel. We get some wildfires and avalanches in the mountains around here, but those events don't usually grow to the size that triggers our involvement.

A new situation has come about, which is why I'm starting this journal. It all started about a week ago, too soon after Christmas for my liking. Two men came to work for an impromptu meeting to talk to us. The first thing I noticed about them when I walked into the conference room was their hair was perfectly combed and in place. The second thing was their suits. They had very crisply pressed black suits and brightly colored silk ties. One had a solid red tie and the other's was solid green. No patterns or paisley, just a bright solid color. Later that night, all I could picture in my mind about them was their ties. I couldn't remember what their faces looked like.

At the meeting, we were told to clear our schedules and make time for them. Over the course of the week, they asked questions and interviewed us about the work we've done. Their questions made me feel uneasy about why they were here. They asked about the scale of disasters we've dealt with recently, examples of how the team worked together under stress, and gave us some off-the-wall scenarios to talk about. They slowly alluded their purpose in being here was about a disaster for us to manage, until they hit us with the big news today.

Because of my job, I get to know about disasters, and coming disasters, before most other people. That's why I know about the one that's coming now. At FEMA, we don't refer to disasters as "doozies", but this one is a doozy. I can't quite comprehend its scale yet and need some time to mentally process it. I have to stop writing because my head hurts. I'll write more later.

2
JOURNAL
The Beginning

It's been a couple of days since my first journal entry. Max and I went skiing last weekend so I could take my mind off work. We took a few runs, but it wasn't enough to distract me. I was preoccupied about this work thing and fell a few times. Max got a kick out of that because he's usually the one falling more. I was going pretty fast one time and kicked up a huge cloud of snow as I tumbled down the slope. After I shook the snow off my jacket and wiped away the melting snow dust on my face, I had to trudge up the hill in my stiff boots to get my skis so I could put them back on. I took Max into the chalet for a hot chocolate before we hit the slopes again. But, enough of that. On to my entry for today.

Okay. Here goes. Take a big breath and let it out, Gene. Shake out the fingers and hands, and just start writing. My fingers are shaking badly from the stress. I hope the writing isn't too jumbled.

I realize my nervousness and reluctance to write about this are silly. It's not like I'm breaking the news to any of you. Anybody who reads this will already know what's happening, or happened, I guess, from your perspective. I'm still having trouble comprehending it, though.

Our group was among the first at FEMA to be briefed on the planet. "On the planet" could sound confusing, but, again, I realize that anyone reading this will already know the exact context. It's history for you, but I'm going to experience it as it happens.

When I say "on the planet", I don't mean we were the first "on Earth" to be briefed. What I mean is we were some of the first to be briefed about the planet that's hurtling toward us. As hard as it is to believe, there's a very large object coming through space toward Earth. It's a planet. That large. Yeah, a big one.

When we grew up, we learned there were nine planets in our solar system, plus other stuff like asteroids and comets. The number changed to eight when Pluto was demoted to a dwarf planet, but that was just a change to a man-made definition. It didn't fundamentally change what the objects in our solar system are. To us, they've been there since before mankind developed, and they'll be there for a long time to come. From our perspective, they're stable and constant, and there's a calming nature about them. They're nothing to worry about. We learn their names, and we learn the Greek and Roman stories they're named after. They become our silent, ever-present friends and confidants. This rogue planet will throw all that security out the window. The cosmos seemed so far away and safe until now.

Ugh. My head hurts already. It's too much to think about all at one time. I should buy stock in aspirin companies for all of the headaches that are coming. That's it for now. I apologize I can't write more. Hopefully, I'll get better at this in the future.

3
EARTH
Falling Apple (Year 1661)

Richard came out from behind his desk. It was a solid, dark walnut piece that had taken six men to carry in and place. The top was covered with neat stacks of papers and manuscripts with several inkwells interspersed among them. One far corner had a darker stain from ink that spilled and hadn't been cleaned up quickly enough.

The office walls were made of dark wooden panels to match the desk, although one couldn't see most of them past the tall book shelves loaded with texts. The large windows behind the desk let in as much light as possible so Richard could see during the day. On overcast days and in the evenings, it was more difficult with only the flames of several lamps to light the desk.

Whenever someone new walked into the office for their first time, they noticed a large woven rug. It seemed out of place on the marble floor as it contrasted with the darkness of the wood decor. The rug was full of radiating yellows, oranges, and reds. It depicted four immense white horses rearing, their taut muscles straining as they pulled Apollo's Sun chariot across the sky. Hooves glinted like gold, wild eyes flashed with lightning, nostrils flared, and their long manes flowed back across their bodies forming clouds in the sky. Richard had spent a year of his earnings when he commissioned the unique piece. He wanted something to dominate the viewer's first impression and subtly convey he was a formidable man.

Richard turned the corner of his desk and walked across the rug to shake James' hand. Today he was wearing a suit with a solid blue tie. Richard's tie was also blue, but a lighter shade. It was important that one's tie was a single color without patterns, and Richard liked to take note of what color the others chose to wear and how silky the material was. He wondered what influenced their decision to select a particular color on any given day.

They exchanged greetings and niceties about the weather and their families. Richard knew James was there for a reason, but wasn't sure what it was. As they walked out the grand marble archway from the main hall at Trinity College, they talked about politics and the end of the fighting with the Spanish, although the war wasn't officially over. When they had walked far enough away from the buildings to not be overheard, James changed the subject.

"You must be wondering the reason for my visit," he said. "It's very simple. We've identified another one."

"Ah," Richard absently replied. "I had been wondering. Who might it be?"

"There's a new scholar to nurture," James said. "His name is Isaac. He'll be in your classes this year. We've watched him for a while and have a high degree of confidence in his abilities, if he is guided well. As in the past, teach him, challenge him, pressure him, and encourage him. When you begin to see returns on his training, we'll begin making investments in his work so we will be able to continue our course. As you know, continuing the work is critical, but we must also remain concealed."

Richard made an irritated mental shrug. He knew what was coming in the future and how vital their efforts were, but the group always seemed to think it necessary to remind him each time they found someone new. With a slight sigh, he let the thoughts float away like a leaf on a stream. "Thank you. I will keep a keen eye out for him," he said. "I appreciate the trust that has been put in me. Please let everyone know I will look after him."

They concluded their business, and walked and talked a little longer. They had dinner together that evening before James began his journey back to his office in London.

4

THE ASTRONAUTS
Cargo Shipments

Beckson was getting ready for the monthly shipment due today. They had done final preparation and verification of the storage location two days ago, and it was open and ready. All it needed was the cargo coming in today's shipment.

The automated ship was on its approach. There was nothing more to do until it landed itself, except monitor it in case there was a problem. He stared at the readout on the screen in front of him as its numbers sequenced up and down. With a sudden start, he flinched and blinked his eyes rapidly after he realized he had been staring at the numbers for five minutes without really seeing them. There had never been a problem with the automatic guidance and piloting system yet, and Beckson was bored. He hunkered down for the wait and played a video game on his cell phone. He couldn't use it as a phone to call anyone, but playing the downloaded games was a way to pass the time.

After the ship made a safe landing (surprise, surprise), he flipped on the intercom radio. "Johnson?" he broadcast.

"Go," was the single word reply. Johnson was not the kind of person who'd be memorialized as one of history's great orators. He was highly competent and exacting in his work, but his communication style was concise, sometimes to the point of being curt.

"Time to suit up, Johnson. I'll meet you at the outside door."

"Copy."

They suited up at the door, depressurized the airlock, and headed out. There was plenty of light from the Sun, but they couldn't see the Earth. In fact, neither of them had seen the Earth since they arrived; a consequence of being on the far side of the Moon.

5

JOURNAL
Good News / Bad News

It snowed 14 inches last night. I had to snowblow the driveway before heading to work. It was a slower commute than normal today, but watching the last light snow come down made it more bearable. A bunch of people were late getting to the office, and Max's school was delayed. On days like this, his bus comes at 9:30 a.m. rather than 7:30 a.m. He likes it because he gets to go back to bed. No such luck for me.

As I was driving, I was wondering what we're going to do about this planet. I mean, they've told us it's coming toward us, but I'm sure they haven't told us everything. Why would they let FEMA know if there wasn't a disastrous side to the situation? We deal with disasters. It would be the only reason to make a special effort to tell us. Maybe they've only told us because they're anticipating a panic from people. I'm sure the public will be scared when they find out.

I tried to focus on driving, but my mind kept coming back to the planet and going over the different kinds of disaster it could cause. Space objects fly by the Earth all the time. We aren't even aware of some of them until they're past. Small meteors hit our atmosphere every day. Sometimes a larger meteor hits the atmosphere and burns up brightly

13

enough to be seen. We see it on the news as video someone accidentally caught on their cell phone or doorbell camera. Something going past the size of a planet would cause a lot of panic. A planet that could hit us would cause a whole lot more panic. Maybe that's why we're involved.

Luckily, we had another meeting with the suit and tie men today. Maybe "luckily" isn't the way I should say it, considering the topic. They told us more about the planet, and it was good news and bad news. The good news is this new planet isn't going to hit us. When they told us that, I immediately thought we'd be out of the "whole lot of panic" scenario. However, they followed it up with the bad news. And the bad news is…really bad. Astrophysicists with super computers have been working on calculations of the planet's path for a long time. Although the planet isn't going to hit us, it's going to come close, really close. Closer than what people call "astronomically" close. So close that we're effed. Seriously effed. At FEMA, we learn how to talk about disasters and how to describe different circumstances and conditions with terminology that's both informative and non-alarming, and the best anybody can come up with to describe this event is "effed". I think we're all still in shock.

From the way they told us and the amount of detail they have, I suspect some people have known about this whole thing for decades. You can't just whip out a space calculation on a super computer with ten minute's notice. Why do you think it suddenly became so urgent to put a man in space in the 1950s, land on the Moon, explore other planets? They said it was an attempt to get us prepared for this. But, prepared for what, exactly?

So, there's a planet coming at us. As I said, the good news is it isn't going to hit the Earth. I'd sure call that good news. That's normally the good news when we talk about celestial objects in our solar system. I was relieved to hear it. The bad news, as bad news has a tendency to do, negated the good news and made the relieved feeling shrivel up and wilt away.

The bad news in this case is worse than the other planet simply coming really close and going past. It's going to be so close the gravity of the two planets is going to interact. They won't collide, but will interact, and the Earth is going to be on the losing end of the clash. They've had astronomers, astrophysicists, and computer scientists working on the measurements and trajectory calculations for a long time. It turns out the planet is going to pass by two times. One not so bad, relatively speaking, and the other a whole lot worse.

The planet's currently traveling in a straight line, but its path on the initial pass is going to be affected by the gravity of the Earth and the Sun. After the initial pass, it's going to start a curve around the Sun and come back. Also, they're predicting the planet will steal away the Moon on its first pass. The Moon will leave us and will end up orbiting the other planet. That's horrible in itself, but then they told us more. The bad news just kept coming. On the second pass, about six months after the first, the two planets get closer, and there's going to be an even bigger interaction. The second interaction is going to affect the new planet's path to such an extent it's going to start orbiting the Sun. As they say, though, physics is physics, even on a planetary scale. (Do they really say that? Who are "they"?) According to the laws of motion, there has to be a reaction to that action. Since the gravity action will be between the Earth and this new planet, the reaction will be to the Earth. I can hardly believe it, but the reaction will be the Earth being thrown out of its orbit.

And that's the bad news. Really, there's a series of bad news after bad news piled on top of a steaming heap of bad news. That's why we're effed. There's no way to survive on Earth if it isn't in its orbit, and there's no way to get seven billion people through space to a new planet. It's not like we can build a ladder between the two planets and have everyone move across in one night. Even if there were a way to move all of humanity, there'd be no way to move billions and trillions of plants, animals, insects, fish, bacteria, and everything else it takes to have a sustainable ecosystem.

But, hey, we've got two years to figure something out, right? No worries. Where's the aspirin?

6
THREE QUEENS
Stephanie's List

Stephanie walked through the grocery store pushing her cart. Her two young children were sitting side by side in the seats by the handle absentmindedly kicking their feet out and back. She was relieved they weren't fighting and crying today. They appeared bigger and rounder than other children in the store because they were bundled in multiple layers of clothes to stay warm. They couldn't afford winter coats.

Her shopping list had been very carefully crafted. The budget was tight, and Stephanie didn't have any room for extras. Each week she took the coupon section from her neighbor's Sunday newspaper after they put it in their trash bin. She would go through it and clip coupons for food they needed. She was embarrassed about it, and tried to sneak out and do it in the dark on Sunday night. The neighbors had come out once or twice while she was there, but Stephanie tried to make it look like she was taking her trash out, too.

Stephanie's shopping included a lot of packaged food. The mass produced food was a cheap option and was easy to get ready. She was always hurrying to get supper ready for when Steve got home because much of her time was taken up by the children. She had frozen lasagna, frozen pizza, and frozen stroganoff meals in the cart. She also had white bread, peanut butter, and jelly for the kids' lunches. There were eggs and bacon for breakfast; Steve liked eggs and bacon.

As she turned the corner of an aisle at the back of the store, Stephanie's eye was drawn to a dented can of chipped beef on the discount shelf. It was still good and was only there because the can was badly dented. She picked it up and contemplated it before putting it back. Although it was tempting, her shopping list was made to match a budget and didn't have room for extras.

As the food was being scanned in the checkout line, Stephanie anxiously watched the total go up. She knew exactly how much money she had and how much she had in coupons. She hoped the total wouldn't be over. Most weeks it was close, but some weeks the total was too much. This was one of those weeks, and she needed to make a decision. What would she take out so she had enough money to pay?

She thought about it quickly as she stood there feeling embarrassed, stifling back sobs with tears welling up in her eyes. Steve's beer wasn't an essential for meals, but she couldn't put it back. He would be too upset by not having any beer and buying a less expensive brand would send him into a fit of rage. Similarly, he had to have enough to eat for dinner and had to have his bacon for breakfast. Finally, Stephanie decided she and the kids would have peanut butter sandwiches without jelly this week. After the cashier deducted the jelly, she had enough money to pay. Some weeks the money was just that tight.

7

THREE QUEENS
Susan's List

Susan walked through the grocery store pushing her cart. She enjoyed this time. The store was so bright, and the quiet background music always made her feel good. The kids were at school, and she had plenty of time, although she sometimes missed the times in the past when they would all go to the store and explore the different food colors and smells together. She casually unzipped her coat and laid it over her purse on the back of the shopping cart.

She was looking for just a few things today. She came to the store every day or two to pick up some fresh food for supper and any other provisions they were running low on. Milk, nut and grains cereal, fruit. Those kinds of things.

Today she was picking up some fresh green beans and a package of chicken. She loved cooking fresh, healthy meals for her family. She hummed a little to the store's background music and swayed back and forth slightly as she pushed her cart down the aisles. She picked a carton of cream out of the dairy cooler and added it into the cart so she could make fresh whipped cream to go with the pie left over from last night.

At the checkout counter, she loaded her choices onto the belt and browsed the magazines as she waited for her turn. She glanced at the candy bars and gum, but didn't take any. She didn't want to have the extra sugar. The cashier finished scanning the groceries, got her attention, and let her know the total. Susan put her credit card into the machine to pay, put the last bag in her cart, and went out to her car to drive home.

8
THREE QUEENS
Karen's List

Karen walked through the grocery store pushing her cart. She didn't have much time because Dodger was still in the car, but she wanted to pick up a few things. Normally, she shopped at the natural food store near her apartment, but this was just a quick stop for one thing.

Although they weren't why she stopped, she idly grabbed an avocado, a lemon, and some greens for dinner tonight. They'd add to the vegan food she already had at home. These were impulse buys in addition to what she was here for, dog food. She went to the pet supply aisle and looked for the natural, wheat-free dog food for Dodger. It was high up the shelves, and she had to stretch to reach up and bring it down. Even though his brand was also at her normal natural food grocery store, she liked to get it at this store to help support the people who worked here.

Karen placed her hemp cloth grocery bags on the belt before the food. She wanted to make sure they were used. To protect her Mother Earth, Karen was always sure to bring her grocery bags into the store each time. She didn't like the thought of using the mass-produced plastic bags from the store with all of the negative environmental impact they had. It made her sad when she thought about the plastic bags floating around Mother's oceans and was glad she wasn't adding to it.

She paid for her small amount of groceries and went out to the car. Karen zipped her coat higher up her neck as she walked through the chilly wind. She had to get back to Dodger before he got too lonely. She was all he had.

9

JOURNAL
More History

The furnace went out today. Jenny called to let me know the house was down to sixty-five degrees after lunch. That was just super news. I had a headache from the morning at work, but called a repair place to get a technician to come out. He got there around 4 p.m. and had to replace the furnace's circuit board. It's fixed, but the house is still heating up. My fingers are a little stiff writing this, but there's some important news to put down.

We had a meeting this morning with more suit and tie men. Why are their ties always a solid color? I wonder if they buy them in bulk and hand them out. Anyway, they clued us in more on the background of the situation. I was right about people knowing about this planet for a long time, but I guessed wrong on the time scale. It hasn't been decades. It's been centuries. Tycho Brahe discovered it in the 1600s when he was doing his measurement of the planets. He kept it secret and removed it from his scientific journals after figuring out it was coming toward us.

You know how they talk about the Illuminati running the world from behind the scenes? It turns out they're real. They're the suit and tie people, although they don't call themselves Illuminati anymore. They've changed their name several times throughout the years to keep their anonymity, but Illuminati is the one that's stuck with all of the stories. They're calling themselves the Briar Patch Group right now.

Stories about Briar Patch (née Illuminati) influencing things in the world are true. It's been made clear to us Briar Patch has been involved with governments throughout the past few hundred years, but they've kept themselves disconnected enough to not be running them directly. They sponsor politicians and have influence of course, but it hasn't always been as nefarious as the stories. They've been keeping the secret of the Planet; keeping it so it isn't forgotten, but also guiding scientific advancement in the hope we'd be far enough advanced when the time came. Briar Patch has been keeping the secret when people have been tempted to reveal it. They told us as a warning in case any of us were thinking about telling anyone. That particular influence <u>has</u> been through nefarious means. They swore us to secrecy and told us not even to tell our families.

Brahe discovered this planet and Briar Patch has been keeping the secret. They've supported some astronomers who explore the region of the sky where the planet is while quietly preventing other astronomers from doing so. The astronomers under their influence remove evidence of the planet from their observations and keep quiet about it. In return, their work continues to get funding. Some occupations and hobbies are inherently dangerous. As it turns out, astronomers, both professional and amateur, have a high accidental death rate. The matter-of-fact way the Briar Patch "ties" told us this information made my blood chill. I'm sure they told us to warn us about the consequences of not keeping quiet. It worked. They scared the hell out of me.

At the same time as hiding the planet, the Briar Patch Group has been applying nudges to scientific and technological advancements. Steam engines, gas engines, rocket engines; submarines, airplanes, space stations; calculators, computers, robotics. Human history has been influenced by inventions that can be used to measure and calculate the Planet's path more precisely. After they were confident in its path and, consequently, how close it would come to us, they came up with the beginnings of a plan to save humanity.

The plan they came up with seems desperate and daring, but what else can we do? It sounds almost silly to talk about, but, again, what else can we do? They've been dealing with it for a long time and have a perspective I don't. Their plan is to have us seed the planet with some life as it comes by, giving it time to work on terraforming during its trip around the Sun. Then we'll move a small number of people to it on the second pass. "People" will survive, but most of us won't. That's why they've told us. They're the thinkers of the concept, and we're the "details and execution" people.

We're lucky because the human race has the knowledge and technology to do this. Rocket technology is so plentiful that private companies are even doing it. And the space station has been used for spacefaring experiments.

Aside from the shocking news about how long Briar Patch has known about the Planet and the lengths they go to keep it secret, the really shocking news from today is they've been stockpiling non-perishable supplies in capsules on the far side of the Moon for the past five years. Five years without any news organizations finding out. That's quite an accomplishment.

10
JOURNAL
Keeping a Secret

I'm afraid something bad has happened. Dale Cainnech didn't show up to work after the weekend. He told me Friday he was taking his family to a cabin in the mountains to get away. Something about his demeanor didn't seem right to me. Normally, he's very calm and steady, but he kept looking around when he was talking about it. He seemed anxious.

There was a report Sunday night on the news about a car that went off an icy corner in the mountains and rolled down the side of the canyon. I thought the wreck on the TV looked a little like his SUV. It had tumbled about 100 feet down the side of the canyon and was very badly damaged.

Everybody at work wondered where Dale was today, but nobody mentioned the accident. I don't think anyone wanted to try to connect the two things. From what he said Friday, I wonder if he took his family to a cabin so he could tell them about the Planet. Did Briar Patch know? Did they cause the accident? Did they do something to him and his family?

I'm starting to wonder if Briar Patch is tracking us. They said they've had to do terrible things in the past to keep the Planet a secret. Is this really what they meant? Part of me doesn't want to believe there are people in the world who will go so far for something they believe in, but another part of me sat in a conference room listening to stern looking men in suits with solid colored ties talk about centuries-old conspiracies and a planet nobody's ever heard of. I may have to adjust my thoughts on what people are capable of.

I hope I'm wrong, but a question is nagging at me. Am I putting Jenny and Max in danger by writing this journal? What am I doing? I just wanted a way to process my thoughts. I figured it would be a way to put them in a cohesive form if I could write them down, rather than being all jumbled up and tumbling around in my head. Was that wrong of me?

Some days I have a tough job and some days I have an easy job. If it's true Briar Patch killed Dale, one of the hardest parts of my job now is at home. They're serious the Planet <u>has</u> to be kept secret. If not, there's going to be mass panic. When the public finds out, there's still going to be mass panic, but life will be better for longer if we can delay when that happens.

Not telling people means I can't tell Jenny and Max. That's what makes my job hard at home. What would I tell them if I could? "I love you guys, but no matter what, we only have two years to live." It's not like we're going to contract a lethal disease or be in a car accident. Those things affect single-digit percentages of the world's population. This is going to affect <u>everyone</u> - our neighbors, our friends, priests, teachers, garbage collectors, tax accountants. The Planet won't discriminate. How could it? It has no concept of the creatures walking around here, and the systems we've devised to differentiate ourselves from each other.

For everyone's safety, my family will find out along with everyone else. I'll have to stand and face the consequences of that choice when the time comes. Whenever it comes, maybe I'll tell them earlier that day. Until then, I need to keep this journal an absolute secret.

While writing the journal, I've been hiding it behind some 70ish-year-old pickled onions on top of one of the dusty wooden shelves in the basement. Other old canned vegetables are on the lower shelves, probably because they're more appealing. Pickled onions. I mean, who pickles onions? My grandfather, that's who. Who keeps 70ish-year-old pickled onions on a shelf in their basement? Me, I suppose. Maybe I'm a bit of a pack rat. Maybe that comes from living in the house you and your dad both grew up in. We never had to clean everything out during a move. I figure nobody will be interested to look behind dusty jars of pickled onions on a dusty shelf for a small journal they don't know exists.

11

JOURNAL
The President's Speech

The government told people last night. Actually, <u>every</u> government told people last night. I'm glad they did. It was killing me to keep the secret. I've been paranoid about being followed by the Briar Patch for weeks. I keep looking in the rear-view mirror when I drive to see if there's a car back there following me. I jump every time I see someone in a dark suit and look to see what kind of tie they're wearing. Three days ago, I thought a blue sports car was following me. I nearly ran into the car in front of me at a stop light because I was looking in the mirror so much. Even so, it stayed behind me until I got to the entrance of the neighborhood. It kept going straight when I turned in, which could have been innocuous or it could have been by design to get me to drop my guard. Either way, I've been a mental wreck about being followed.

As I said, the world leaders went on the television simultaneously yesterday to tell everyone. Maybe they couldn't agree on who should be the one to deliver the news so they all did it at the same time. They did it in their own countries and on their own TV networks. I expected them to wait longer, but they showed worldwide unity by doing it at one time. And my nerves are glad they did.

As planned, I told Jenny and Max about 30 minutes before the President went on the air. They didn't take it well, and there was a lot of loud yelling coming from our house. Jenny was especially mad I'd kept it from her, and we hadn't told her parents. Max was mad, but more so because he was following Jenny's lead. He's only ten and doesn't quite have the maturity to process the news on a level higher than shock at the moment.

Jenny's made it clear I'm not on her list of favorites right now. Like most men, I've been in the doghouse before. This time I think I'm in the dog's outhouse, at the bottom of the steamy hole. Actually, from where I am I think I can see the bottom of the outhouse somewhere above me. It looks nice there. I'd rather be there.

I looked up a copy of the President's speech so I could remember it later. Here's what he said.

"My fellow Americans. Let me begin by expressing my love for you, for this country, and for the world. I am joining you tonight from the Oval Office and am addressing you simultaneously along with all world leaders.

"This is the most difficult speech I've given in my life. As your President, it is my pleasure to give you good news, but the burden of bad news is also mine. At times like this, it's a terrible burden. As much as I would prefer not to be standing here talking to you tonight, I would not wish it on anyone else. For the next few minutes, it may be difficult to listen to what I'm telling you, but please listen to everything I have to say.

"Our country, and our world, is facing a crisis unlike any

we've ever known. I've come before you to let you know there are significant events unfolding for the Earth. These events have been unfolding since the time when our solar system was forming. In biblical times, they were happening. They were happening when Galileo was mapping the heavens. During exploration, colonization, and revolutionary times, they've been happening. As long as the Earth has been circling the Sun, they've been happening. On a celestial scale, they've been progressing steadily. And, unfortunately for us, they're coming to a conclusion in our time.

"In our prehistory, Earth has survived several catastrophic events. Our Moon was formed when a planet called Theia struck the Earth billions of years ago. An asteroid struck the Earth 60 million years ago and caused the extinction of the dinosaurs.

"This next part will be difficult to hear, but please listen to it all. It is my ill-fated obligation to tell you about a new planet coming toward us. It isn't orbiting our Sun, but is coming through space in our direction.

"Your first thought might be to wonder if it's going to hit the Earth. Let me assure you it isn't. I want to repeat, it isn't going to hit us. However, it will come close enough to interact with the Earth. It's going to pass close by us, circle around the Sun, and pass by again. The second time it passes it'll be much closer. Close enough, in fact, that it's going to affect how we're orbiting around the Sun. Sadly, I have to tell you the Earth is going to leave its orbit around the Sun. At the same time, the new planet will be captured by the Sun and will replace ours.

"Like the Earth currently, this planet will orbit in what's called a "habitable zone" around the Sun. It will be habitable. For some time, we've been making plans to transition some colonists and resources from Earth to this new planet. It won't be an easy task, but it will ensure humanity will continue to survive.

"As of this moment, your governors are in your home states being briefed in detail about the situation. Earlier today, I signed an executive order declaring a national emergency in order to activate the armed forces and the National Guard to provide security and stability in the country. We'll be withdrawing our troops from their stations abroad and will be tightening our borders in the coming months. Our resources will be nationalized so they may be distributed fairly and equitably. As we've done in the past, we'll work together as a nation to accomplish our future goals.

"In the coming months and years, we'll all be tested to our limits. But, I know the American people. My people. Our people. We have always pulled together to help each other in times of crisis, and we will do it again now. We will confront this situation as we always have, and will demonstrate to the world, as we have in the past, the true spirit of this country.

"I pray for your welfare and ask you to pray for each other. God bless you. God bless your families. God bless the United State of America. And God bless this Earth."

12
THREE QUEENS
Stephanie's Calm

Stephanie turned off the television and sobbed gently. Although outwardly it might have appeared she was sad, she felt neither sad nor happy about the news. She felt content and calm, like a giant weight had been lifted from her shoulders. She was okay with the news she was going to die in a little while. She accepted it and welcomed it like an exciting new friend and a comfortable old friend at the same time. She was ready for her life to be over. She wanted it to be over.

Steve braced his hands on the edge of their small kitchen table and pushed hard. The legs of his chair groaned loudly against the yellowed linoleum floor as he pushed it back. He stood up and walked out of the apartment without saying a word. Stephanie, who had frozen when she heard the low pitched squeal of the chair, untensed her muscles and stopped holding her breath. *At least,* she thought to herself, *he didn't hit me on the way out.* She only had to worry about when he came home.

Stephanie hated being there. Steve hit her more now than when they were first married. She stayed because she didn't have any place else to go. They had moved soon after the wedding, and she didn't have any family in the area. In addition, she didn't have any skills to get a job if she did leave. She only finished her last semester of high school and graduated because her mom had sat at the kitchen table with her night after night to make sure she studied. Her kids were so young she couldn't leave them alone to go to work anyway. Steve didn't hit the kids, but she knew he would if she left without taking them with her.

Stephanie gently slid the chair back under the table and cleaned up the dishes in the kitchen. If they were sitting in the sink or on the counter when Steve came home, she knew he'd be upset and things would be worse. When the dishes were finished and dried, she went to the kids' bedroom. She shuffled her feet as she crossed the room so she didn't step on any of their toys, crawled into the tiny bed they shared, and cuddled them close. They didn't wake up, but fidgeted in a restless sleep. She cried some more, and the gentle shaking of her sobs seemed to calm the children. They were used to hearing their mother crying while they slept.

Her crying ended quickly as a wave of relief flowed over her mind. She resolved to stay for, w*hat had the President said, the coming months and years?* She would stay with the children to protect them, but had no interest in trying to go to this new planet and no delusions her life could be better there. Why would she want to live on another planet with more of the same? She just wanted things to end and was glad they would.

13
THREE QUEENS
Susan's Calm

Susan turned off the television and sobbed gently. She stood in the living room entrance where she had watched the speech, and tried to collect her thoughts. The news was overwhelming, but she felt at ease. She didn't want to believe it. The President's words echoed in her head and terrified her. *There's a huge planet coming to wipe us out*, she thought to herself. *What does it all mean? What will happen to us? To the children?*

Roger stood up from the sofa and walked over to hug her. She stood there and cried in his arms. Her shoulders shook as she sobbed. He held her gently, but tightly, and let her let it all out. She could tell he was also crying, but was trying to hide it to be strong for her.

He sniffled a little after a while and said, "We'll be alright. We have each other and our friends. And we have our faith in the Lord. I love you and the kids more than anything. We can treasure every day we have left."

His words helped Susan start to feel better. They had such a happy life she didn't want it to end. If it had to end, though, she'd appreciate it as much as she could until the end.

14
THREE QUEENS
Karen's Calm

Karen turned off the television and sobbed gently. She didn't want the Earth to die. She loved the natural world she lived in and didn't want to see it end. Karen spent her weekends and vacation time hiking with Dodger in the mountains and climbing to the summit of nearby Mount Hope. Sometimes they went to watch the sunset, sometimes they got up early and went for the sunrise, and sometimes they went to simply look out across the sky to where the horizon met the fields far to the east.

Mount Hope wasn't the real name of the mountain, but all of the locals called it that due to the way it glowed when the light of the morning sunrise struck the rocky faces. There was a unique mineral composition within the stone of one section of the mountain range that caused the glowing affect. At times, it was like the gentle golden radiance of a gilded cathedral dome. At other times, it was as if the rock was afire with scintillating patterns of yellow, orange, and red.

Dodger heard her crying softly, got up, and walked over to nuzzle against her leg. Karen put her hand down and patted his head. Despite the sudden unexpected change in the state of the world, his dark brown fur was as soft as always. She bent down to grab the fur on the sides of his head and gently shook it back and forth. Then she circled her hands over his ears and under his chin. She hugged him and laid her head against his neck.

We'll be okay, Karen determined. If Dodger didn't know what would be happening, she wouldn't change their routine. She wanted to enjoy the mountains, streams, and meadows for as long as they could.

Mother Earth was going to be dying. Karen reasoned her life came from Mother Earth, and it belonged to Her. Karen's life would end with her Mother's.

15

JOURNAL
After the President's Speech

After the President's speech, people were left in shock. We had talked about it at work beforehand and couldn't decide what the reaction would be. They could barely see the Planet in the sky if they looked in the right place, buildings weren't falling down around them, grocery store shelves were still well stocked, and people's basic needs were being met. We knew people would have questions and would need to be given more information, though. That type of news doesn't fall under my group, fortunately. It was up to other parts of the government and the media. We thought most people would ignore the news because it would be overwhelming and there wasn't an immediate change to their everyday lives. We were wrong.

Immediately after the speech, people took to the streets, and there was massive rioting around the world. It was awful. It's been going on for days. It was like cities were under siege from within. The news showed footage of the destruction; store windows smashed, businesses burning, even neighborhoods on fire. Other footage showed people trying to help others who had blood streaming down their faces and stained shirts. One news station was live at a scene when the mob changed directions. They tried to run, but it overtook them. Jenny and I watched in horror as the reporters and people trying to aid the injured were senselessly beaten on live television. The station cut out soon after it started, thank goodness. So far, tens of thousands of people have been killed because some of the crowds don't care what they do to people who are in their way. More than that have been injured.

The rioting is causing billions of dollars of damage to property and has nearly shut down parts of the economy. Stores are only getting deliveries when they can get through. The army was sent out domestically to stop the violence. They're escorting food deliveries from farms to processing plants, and from processing plants to grocery stores. After the delivery trucks get to the stores, they stay to protect the stores from rioters and stealing. In general, the protection efforts work during the day, but not at night. Hopefully, after everything is looted and broken, people will have had enough and it'll fade away.

There's been rioting near where we live, too. Luckily it hasn't come to our neighborhood, though. People start arriving at dusk in the business district about two miles away from the house. Small groups on a street merge into larger groups. Large groups merge into crowds that fill the streets for several blocks. At some point, someone or something breaks a window or kicks down a door, and the rioting is triggered. The crowds need a spark each night to set them off, and some people go to provide it.

My group's first task was to move all of the families of anyone remotely connected to the government peacekeeping forces. We had planned for this, but hadn't foreseen needing to begin so quickly. They were all moved to bases so they'd be safe from the violence happening in the streets. Something we've learned in the past is the people holding the line will do a better job if they know their family is safe. If not, some will abandon their jobs and go to their family.

The debates started right away after the President's speech. The first one came from the environmentalists. They questioned whether we ought to go to the new planet at all. Their argument was we've messed up the Earth and will mess up this new place, too. Although the argument hasn't stopped coming up, most people have dismissed it. They'd rather be alive on the Planet than worry about polluting it.

The next debate was the big one on everyone's mind. Who gets to go? The debate is academic, but people don't realize that. News organizations, non-profit groups, and public sentiment aren't going to be contributing to that decision. Briar Patch has their list, I'm sure, but they're holding those cards close to their vest. They probably have plans in place for their own people in addition to ones for the government.

The government is going to be building and sending ships, but they'll have limited space. They announced there'll be some selected spots and a nationwide lottery for the rest. I bet the only people over 30 who will get to go will be politicians, religious leaders, and billionaires. God, that combination's going to be a mess. I think when they announce the lucky people from the lottery, the world's going to explode into rioting. The ones we had after the President's speech will look tame compared to what'll happen when people's thin hope for survival is dashed.

There was an unexpected result of the President's speech, too. My team and I didn't expect it, anyway. The private space companies posted all of their information on the internet. All of the plans and designs they have for rockets, capsules, space suits, materials, launch pads, equipment, software, etc. They posted everything. The tech giant CEOs with the private space companies got together and decided the best way to give the most people a chance was to share their information. They were all going to have their own spaceships anyway, so why not let others try?

It's quite a quandary. Of course the billionaires are going to make it. They have all of the resources to build their own ships that'll take their families and maybe some other people. Their money won't be any good on the new planet, but it won't matter at that point. They'll be there, and they'll be alive. Going forward, a lot of decisions will be made around trying to stay alive.

While many people took to rioting in the streets, there was another place devastated by the President's news: the stock market.

The news about the planet came as a complete shock to companies and investors around the world. They immediately began pulling their money out of the markets and putting it into commodities. The stock market dropped so severely it triggered the automatic safety rules and trading was suspended. When the suspension was lifted, the markets dropped again, and the next level of trading suspension kicked in. This process continued each time the markets were re-opened.

To shore up their stock, companies used their free cash to buy the stock being sold. That could only last so long, though, and companies stopped buying their own stock as they forecasted running out of money.

That was when the crash stopped. You can only sell a stock if someone is willing to buy it. Investors weren't buying, and companies weren't buying. Nobody was buying. Everyone left with stock after the initial sell-off couldn't do a thing. The retirement account I contributed to each month is worthless. It's not like it's going to matter. Nobody's going to need retirement money in the future, anyway.

16

JOURNAL
About Arcas

I realize if you're reading this journal, you know all about Arcas, but I want to write about the planet itself. Writing here helps my mind process the information. Maybe it'll also provide some perspective about the Earth your ancestors came from.

Arcas is the name Tycho Brahe gave to the planet he discovered. I haven't been able to make myself write its name until now. Using its name makes it more real and more of something I have to acknowledge and accept.

The story behind the name Arcas has to do with the Greek gods. (Greece was an ancient country on Earth.) Arcas was the son of Callisto and Zeus, the king of the Greek gods. To protect Callisto and Arcas from his jealous wife, Hera, Zeus turned them both into bears, grabbed them by the tails, and flung them into the sky where they became the constellations, Ursa Major and Ursa Minor, the Great Bear and the Little Bear. I guess the name seemed fitting to Brahe since Arcas is sailing toward us. I doubt he knew the irony, however, Arcus would eventually fling the Earth into the sky.

We've been able to learn quite a bit about the make up of Arcas.

Living there is going to be a change for whomever makes it. To start with, it has one and a half times the gravity of Earth. That means a 175 pound person will weigh around 260 pounds there. That's going to be a big adjustment. Many people, us included, have gone out and bought weight vests. They're wearing them to strengthen their muscles. Smart people have also bought ankle and wrist weights. The President said some people are going to be picked to go to Arcas, but nobody knows who that'll be for sure so everyone is hoping it'll be them.

Arcas is a rocky planet and has about the same average density as Earth. Its circumference is a little under 60,000 km, compared to Earth's circumference of 40,000 km. It's a much bigger ball than the Earth. That'll take some getting used to, as well, but it'll take a long time before the whole place is colonized and populated like the Earth is now.

Arcas is spinning on an axis, and it has a magnetic field. That implies the core is pretty similar to Earth. There must be a solid metal core spinning inside the planet to make a magnetic field. Even the Moon has a liquid core so I guess it's not uncommon for planetary objects. That's lucky for us. Having a magnetic field means it's been protected from charged interstellar particles that would otherwise scour the surface clean. Like on Earth, the particles are directed by the magnetic field to the Arcas north and south poles.

Because it's been protected, the surface of Arcas has a layer of dust, like many objects in our solar system. They call it regolith. It doesn't have anything like the dirt we're used to because it hasn't had billions of years of time, water, and wind eroding the surface. And there's nothing like organic soil. Something it does have, though, is ice. With the magnetic field protection, compounds erupting out from inside just flow onto the surface and freeze, like the lava volcanoes on Earth, the watery cryovolcanism of Jupiter's Europa moon, and the sulfur volcanoes on Jupiter's Io moon. The surface is pockmarked from meteorite strikes and is covered by broken up lava and regolith. Not only does it have rocks and dust, but it also has other frozen compounds that would be gases on Earth. As it gets closer to the Sun, those things will start to melt. Liquids will form lakes or oceans, and the ones that are gases will form an atmosphere. It won't be easy to live there, but it'll be possible.

So there it is. We're walking around wearing weights just in case. If we get to go, that is. We have all of the weights we'll need, but will be building them up slowly. We need to take our time because we can't have our arms and legs suddenly weigh $1\frac{1}{2}$ times as much and hope to get anything done. I don't even think I could hold my arm up to write with a pencil if I did it all at once.

17
JOURNAL
Theology at Risk

The debates going on about Arcas have come to my work. As with any employer, we have people from all kinds of backgrounds. Being in a large city, we have our fair share of differences. We've been having talks about the pollution argument. Not in our meetings, mind you. We don't allow distractions when it's working time, but there's time to talk during the day and at lunch time.

I can see the argument about leaving Arcas alone so we don't give it man-made problems, but I'm not on that side. I'm on the side of kicking the can down the road. Arcas is such a large planet, there'll be so few people and no established industry. It'll take hundreds of years before any reasonable amount of pollution crops up. As the industry builds, there's a huge chance of repeating the factory pollution problems we have here, but I hope the Arcasians will learn about Earth's history and learn lessons from our first go-around.

One of the more interesting discussions happening is related to theology. It's the age-old question of whether there is a God or not. Boiling the debate down to its most basic essence, it's this: is Arcas an act of God or an act of science? It's a tough question and has been polarizing. The science-y types and theologians are at odds.

Even within the "act of God" camp, people are falling into several divisions. Some say God has sent Arcas to punish us. They're the ones who equate bad events as being a punishment from God. When they're questioned about why they're also being punished, they don't have a good answer, though. I think they're saying humanity as a whole is being punished for the wicked deeds of the majority. They've accepted their fate that they won't survive this event.

Another group of believers say God has sent Arcas as a way to save us. They've borrowed part of the "we've poisoned the Earth" argument from the environmentalists. They've taken it in another direction, though, by saying God has sent Arcas as a do-over. Although most of humanity will be gone, a small number will be saved and will be able to start over with a new planet, like a new Garden of Eden. This group also accepts their fate because they know "God's creation will continue". A lot of them secretly hope they'll be able to go to Arcas. They want to be the ones to start afresh in an unspoiled Eden.

Finally, some say God set this in motion a long time ago as a test to see if we'd rise to the challenge. They look at it as a trial from God; He gave us enough time to advance as a civilization that could overcome the trial. They're actually excited about Arcas. (I'm not.) Like the second group, they hope they'll be the ones picked to go to Arcas, but they're eager to help out as much as possible. Even if they don't get to go, they want to help those who will.

I've heard these different views brought up often at work. People are adamant about their own belief. The arguments have gotten heated at times, to the point we've had to break up some scuffles over it. Whether they can recognize it in themselves or not, people are feeling a desperation they've never had to deal with before. The fact that Arcas is steadily coming closer is a constant thought in the back of everyone's mind.

With Arcas coming, many people are questioning their religion. Does God exist? Why is this happening? Am I being punished? Do I deserve this? Is there anything after death? Will I go to Heaven? Will I go to Hell? Jenny and I haven't been immune to this. We've questioned God and His plan along with everyone else. We've never been strongly religious in the past, but something like this turns your mind to it more.

No matter what the religion is, it doesn't have lessons or scriptures that cover this exact situation. Some say it's a sign of the apocalypse or Armageddon. I suppose it could be since the world as we know it will be destroyed; it'll become a cold, dead planet floating through space. Unlike Armageddon, though, there isn't going to be a final battle between good and evil. Well, maybe there will be in a way. There's going to be a lot more rioting and probably worse before it's all over.

To their credit, the world's religious leaders have stepped in. They've been in front of their followers constantly. They have daily Masses, or whatever they refer to their services as. The Pope leads a Mass at different times around the clock, and the Vatican broadcasts it worldwide. Other religious leaders are also broadcasting theirs. They want to comfort their followers and keep them positive. The Pope preaches about the absolute charity of Jesus, and His suffering for us. We're going to need this more and more as time goes on. People will need something to relieve their stress and confusion over what is happening and why. It'll help them through their grief.

18
JOURNAL
My Job

I haven't really explained why my team at FEMA was told about Arcas early. I apologize for that. They told us because we're experts on emergencies, we're experts on planning, and we're one of the best teams at FEMA for it. We have plans for all kinds of natural and unnatural disasters. Part of our normal job is to think and plan. We execute our plans, take our experience, and rethink our plan for the next time. Some disasters are theoretical because they haven't happened yet. For the theoretical ones, we take time to poll ourselves on the hypotheticals and re-brainstorm ideas. That makes us somewhat unique.

Our unique job also means we could start making plans for Arcas as part of our normal routine and stay under the radar. We did until the President gave his speech. After the speech, the cat was out of the bag and we didn't have to hide what we were doing anymore. If Dale had waited a little longer to tell his family, they might all be alive still. We don't have to hide our work because nobody's really concerned about what our small group is up to now anyway. They're all too busy rioting.

Our job in this is to help plan and prepare for the transfer from Earth to Arcas. Briar Patch has come up with some plans, but have mostly been working on developing the technology to get to Arcas. They've asked us to come up with the ideas and logistics for what to transfer and how to make it a viable environment. It has to be a very comprehensive plan. Arcas isn't going to have anything other than some water, atmosphere, and lots of rocks. We have to prepare the environment and think of all of the skills, tools, knowledge, and trades that have to go to ensure humanity won't go extinct after we get there.

19
JOURNAL
Sloths Aren't Always Cute

Despite the riots, it's been a very nice summer so far. There's been plenty of rain, and the flowers in the mountains are still blooming. We've been able to take some drives up through the mountains on the weekends to our favorite picnicking place. It's a spot we found a few years ago while taking a drive to look at the fall leaves. We've gone back to it many times over the past few years. The highway canyon opens to a small valley with a meadow and a pond with some trees on one side. The pond is fed by the stream that runs down the canyon and out the other end of the little valley. Every once in a while a few deer poke their heads out of the stand of trees on the far side of the pond. We take a blanket to spread out in the shade for a relaxing time. Sometimes Max and I throw a frisbee after we're done eating.

I've noticed something strange at work lately. It seems like people haven't been showing up on time to meetings. It's unusual because our group culture has always been to be on time for meetings. Now, people are sauntering in five to ten minutes late with an excuse about traffic or how they lost track of time talking with someone on another floor. Then they flop into their chairs and have other excuses for not having their assignments done. I don't get it. Although I understand Arcas is going to make everyone depressed, if we don't make progress on our plans, we're going to jeopardize the future of the human race.

I don't know if it's because it's summer or if there's something else going on. Is the team bored with what we're doing? Maybe they aren't taking it seriously because there's more than a year to go. I'll have to keep an eye on this and make sure it doesn't get out of hand.

20

JOURNAL
Sloths Really Aren't Cute

The laziness at work has been too much, and I had to say something this week. Nobody was coming to work before 10 a.m., and most of them had left for home by 3 p.m. Half of the people thought it was appropriate to wear Hawaiian shirts to work all week long. It was absolutely ridiculous. I could tell from the looks on the faces of the Briar Patch Group "ties" they didn't like the new look at all. They're still coming around with their monochromatic ties and pressed shirts. Their demeanor is so stiff I think they press their ties in addition to their shirts.

It wasn't easy to crack the whip, but the project had ground to a halt. We missed every milestone for the past two weeks, and I hadn't seen half the team in any meetings. I couldn't believe I had to go to people's offices and physically drag everyone into the large meeting room to talk to them all at once. That wasn't easy. Some didn't want to get up, and I literally pushed their chairs down the hall with them sitting in them. They pushed back during the meeting about having to work. People were saying it didn't matter because the Earth was dead anyway. They said it's such a nice summer we should all go out and enjoy the last of our days. Well, the Earth isn't dead yet, everyone is counting on us to succeed, and there's plenty of summer for the next month.

There's been some change in attitude since I chewed everyone out. It wasn't easy to bring their minds back to the work, but this is some of the most important work we've ever done. We're not doing it for ourselves; we're doing it for the rest of the world. We're doing it for the future. It's not easy to explain that to someone and have them fully comprehend. I don't know if it worked for the long haul or not. Time will tell, but people are working again for now.

21
EARTH
Baily Begins (Year 1798)

As he walked down the streets of London one morning, Francis found himself detoured from his normal route several times. At one corner, a wagon had tipped. Its spilled load blocked the street, and he turned left rather than going straight. At another corner, an excessively loud group of children were playing a game, and he turned right to avoid them.

In the middle of one block, a large limestone block crashed to the sidewalk immediately in front of Francis, causing him such a start he stumbled backwards and fell.

"Oh, my goodness! I'm terribly sorry, sir," a man's voice said from the steps next to him. "Are you hurt?"

"No, only my overabundant pride. But, I say, what was that?"

"There are workers making repairs up above. I assure you I'm going to have strong words with them. Their clumsiness could have crushed you." Helping Francis up, the man continued, "Please, come inside and let's get that dirt off your jacket."

"Oh, thank you, but I'm nearly late for my appointment and must be going. It's only a little dust, after all."

The man held Francis strongly by the elbow, and ushered him up the steps and through the door before he realized what was happening. "No, sir. I insist on compensating you for this unfortunate incident. That other appointment can wait. Your appointment inside is more important."

Francis barely had time to register the man's odd comment about an appointment before he was whisked through a sitting room, past a dining room where several gentlemen sat at tables conversing and eating, and into an ornate office.

The office was well lit with several paintings of sunflowers on the walls. The far end of the room had a neat desk with two cushioned chairs in front. The yellows and oranges of the sunflower paintings complemented the colors of a large rug on the floor. It's once bright colors and depiction of horses pulling a flaming sun chariot were faded. The surface was worn from being walked across for years. Francis's keen eyesight noticed a few small burns in one corner, he supposed from fallen ashes of a smoker who once sat at a table located there.

Distracted by his analysis of the rug, Francis forgot about the manner he arrived in the office. "You have an exquisite rug, sir," he said to the man sitting behind the desk.

"Thank you, Mr. Baily," the man said. He wore a dark suit and a pale yellow tie. "It's very old, and I'm quite proud of it, but I'm afraid it's seen better days. Still, it has great sentimental value for us here at the Journeymans' Club.

"I hope my associate, Sidney, treated you well when he invited you in. Mr. Baily, I summoned you here so I could offer my condolences over the recent death of your friend and fellow astronomer, Mr. Brian Thomas. We thought he had a promising career in front of him. And as you know, one of his interests was mapping a particular section of the sky."

"Thank you, Mister… I'm sorry, I didn't catch your name. I sincerely apologize if we've met previously, but your name escapes me. Mister…?" Francis stammered, his voice trailing off. "Wait," he paused again. "Did you say 'Summoned me?'"

"Yes," he answered, "and you may call me Dean."

Francis Baily was confused and off guard, but tried his best to remain a stoic Englishman. "Very well, Mr. Dean. Thank you for your sympathies. My friend Mr. Thomas was a healthy young man. The doctors are baffled as to how his heart stopped.

"I find myself confused, however. He died just yesterday evening. If I may ask, how is it you came to know about his death so soon, and of his work?" Francis asked curiously.

"We'll have time to get into that later if you want," Dean replied. He had, however, no intention of speaking about it again.

"It's been only a year or two since you've been back from touring the unsettled parts of the Colonies." He stopped and corrected himself, "Please forgive me, they call themselves the United States of America now. Is that correct? It must be nice to be in a civilized country after being away for a couple of years."

He continued, "Mr. Baily, it's my great pleasure to be able to extend a wonderful offer to you. If you accept, your research programs will be funded permanently. As you know well, funding is vitally important to a researcher such as yourself.

"My colleagues and I move quickly when the situation warrants it. We gave this opportunity to Mr. Thomas yesterday, but he decided to…" Dean paused slightly and looked directly at Francis before continuing in a more serious voice, "…pass. If you accept our offer, your proposals will be funded, and you'll be given Mr. Thomas's research notebooks to confirm his latest theories and add a final credit to his career."

Again, he continued without giving Francis time to reply, "The only thing we ask in return with this offer is that you verify these coordinates." With that statement, he slid a piece of paper inscribed with a string of numbers across the desk.

"Those are coordinates Mr. Thomas was examining when he incorrectly thought he discovered an object. I can assure you there is nothing unusual at those coordinates."

Then he leaned forward, lowered his voice, and continued in a somber tone, "You will attest to this fact if the time ever comes when verification is necessary for the world. Until such a time, your research will prosper."

Francis took the paper, looked at the numbers, and said, "I'm sorry, sir. Your funding is a wonderful prospect, but how could I possibly agree to those conditions without first examining the coordinates for myself?"

Dean expected this question and was prepared. "Mr. Baily," he leaned back farther in his chair and made a flourishing wave in the air with his hand, "there are times when you have to make decisions based on faith." Then he held a finger up and shook it, "Not religious faith, mind you, but faith in the other person you're dealing with. In our case, faith is a two way street. I've accepted on faith that you're an honorable man and will abide by the terms I've proposed for the foreseeable future. You, deducing what you may about me from our short conversation, will have to accept my assertion on faith."

He lied and said, "For both of us, a great portion of our faith in the other has to be blind. I assure you, there will be time enough for you to view the coordinates later. However," placing his open palm on his chest and then gesturing to Francis, "as is mine, your faith in this matter will have to be based blindly."

Dean rested back and spoke again in a more chipper tone. "You're a smart chap. A pleasant fellow. Please, take some time to think over our offer. You may enjoy lunch here on my account." Motioning to Sidney who had been standing by the door, "Sidney here will show you to the dining room and see to your needs.

"But, I'm afraid I'll need your decision before you leave the club today. Being a smart fellow, I hope you don't decide to pass as well." The way he emphasized the word "pass" made Francis cringe slightly.

Feeling a sweaty chill run down his spine as he stood up, a stunned Francis Baily was led from the room and escorted to the dining room he passed on the way in. Several exquisite looking dishes of food were placed on the table in front of him. He laid his napkin across his lap, idly picked up a gold plated fork to examine it, and hesitated.

He thought about the bizarre morning he had and mulled over the conversation from the past few minutes. *How had he found himself on this street? How had he ended up in this club? What was he being asked to do? Could he accommodate the request if he accepted?*

These were some of the least worrisome questions running through his mind. The color drained from his face and his eyes opened wider in shock as he suddenly comprehended the subtle threat conveyed by the way Dean had spoken about Brian Thomas's death. *Had Thomas been killed? What would happen to himself if he refused? Would he be allowed to leave this club alive?*

Francis finished his thoughts and came to a decision. He took a long breath, let it out slowly, and smiled slightly. With his fork, he flaked a piece from the fish on the nearest plate, put it in his mouth, and began enjoying the best meal of his life.

22
JOURNAL
Art Speaks

Max brought home some of his art projects from school today. They aren't making much new art because the teachers aren't getting new supplies from the schools. Money has been "reallocated" to other areas of government.

I like his art. There was a painted mask; a landscape scene of blue mountains, orange trees, and a green sun made out of ripped construction paper; and a small piece of pottery shaped like a... dolphin? (I wonder, do you even know what a dolphin is?) I squirreled away the mountain with my journal. I like that he didn't feel constrained to make things their natural colors. I figure it'll help cheer me up when I'm feeling depressed about Arcas.

Max's art got me to thinking about artwork in general. I know we need to be planning supplies to transfer to Arcas, but someone has to think about art. It'll be important to take some of the artwork from Earth to preserve our history and culture. I'm glad I won't be in charge of picking what will go and what will be left behind. There's so much great art by the old masters, but also modern artists. What can we take and what can we leave while conscientiously staying aligned with our principles as a society?

My initial thought was about the ceiling of the Sistine Chapel. It's one of the greatest art pieces in history, but it's massively large and heavy, and would be too delicate to move. Then my mind turned to Michelangelo's David, the Venus de Milo, the Winged Victory of Samothrace, and the sculptures of Rodin. The full versions of them are incredibly heavy. It's not my decision, but I don't think we can justify taking such large and heavy works. We could roll up and send most of the paintings in the Louvre in a capsule occupying the same space as one statue and adding much less weight. Yes, I realize rolling the paintings might damage them, but we also have to consider the cost-benefit of how things are sent. The cost of taking paintings out of their frames and rolling them versus the benefit of being able to fit more in a certain space.

Paintings and photography might be the majority of the art that's sent. There'll be pictures of the artwork that doesn't get sent, and stories about them, but that doesn't have the same effect on a person as standing in front of a piece of art and viewing it.

Then I also think about how music, dance, and even fashion are parts of our artistic culture. It's all so depressing to think about how many enriching things will be left behind. Will the people on Arcas have time to remember the different styles of high heel shoes? Walking down the street in a large city here is sometimes an art experience in itself. Then again, with their different gravity, will people on Arcas even care?

23

JOURNAL
Power on Arcas

We've had some problems with electric power recently. As Arcas gets closer, parts of our country's infrastructure are under stress. Like my continuing struggle with my staff, many people have simply stopped going to work; they don't see the point of continuing to work when they have such a short time to live. Fewer people working means fewer people at water and power plants, and to maintain lines. We're down to having reduced power during the day and even less at night. The whole city's in a constant brownout. It really makes it hard to work, and things are slowing down. The office gets hot during the day because the air conditioner has been turned off. We open windows at night to help it cool down and close them in the morning to try to keep cool as long as possible.

It's harder for Max to go to school now. I feel bad about it. He's going to be living every kid's dream of not having school, but he's also not going to be getting an education. Our education system has helped our society and economy grow out of an agricultural one into what it is today. If we stop teaching the children, we might regress. I understand that education won't happen once Arcas is here and the Earth is going away, but it's important to keep some routine things going. It's important to keep a communal purpose and motivation. The mental distraction won't hurt, either.

Speaking of power, the power situation on Arcas is bleak. Electricity, I mean. Since there's never been any life there, it won't have any fossil fuels. No oil for oil wells. No natural gas for gas wells. Nothing. We're going to have to rely on other energy sources for power. It's possible there'll be enough water on the surface for some hydroelectric power. We won't know about that for a long time, though. We're counting on there being enough atmosphere for us to breathe, so that could also provide some wind power. If there isn't enough, this is all moot.

The Arcasians can eventually set up wind generators, but the power sources that are our best bet at the beginning are solar and nuclear. There'll definitely be solar power available. We just need to take solar panels; lots of solar panels. And lots of batteries. Since they're heavy, the idea is to take 25-30% of the panels and batteries we think we'll need in the hope we'll eventually be able to mine the materials to make more.

Nuclear power is the basket we're putting most of our eggs into. You can get the most power out of the smallest amount of materials, and it lasts for a long time. Every ounce of weight we shoot between the planets costs thousands of dollars. We have to be prudent about it. We can get the most power per dollar from nuclear, so we'll spend the money on it.

Since we're planning for power, an issue we have to worry about is what's going to be using the power. Most of our cars, trucks, construction tools, cranes, planes, etc. are gas and diesel fueled. But, that's another area where Briar Patch's technology fostering has come into play. Companies have been building electric vehicles for a few years and working on the mechanics of them so we have some good experience with viable large electric motors. One billionaire even launched his electric car into space. Maybe he knew about Arcas and sent it there. If so, I doubt it landed on its wheels when it went down. Ha! The first car accident on Arcas was a self-driving car.

Anyway, every large vehicle will have to be electric. Even small tools will have to be electric. Luckily, there have been more of those developed. Heck, I even have a bunch in my garage. If I can have an electric lawnmower, trimmer, drill, chop saw, and snow blower, we can certainly get a lot of those to Arcas. And, I'm telling you right now, FEMA won't crash them. Take that, self-driving car!

In order to use the power we generate on Arcas, we have to ship all of the power infrastructure there. Power lines, poles, connectors, insulators, regulators, transformers. Everything. And the tools to put it all together. There's so much we have to send. We even have to send the molds to make more tools to replace broken ones, and the plans for new molds for when the molds break. It feels so overwhelming at times. We have to send everything. Tools, knowledge, arts, science. Everything.

With all the power generator equipment in addition to everything else that has to be sent, we've got to be judicious about the amount of materials we send. The proportions of supplies are very difficult decisions to make. We have to try to balance the variety with the quantity. If we're not careful and send too little of something critical, we could doom the settlers before they get started.

One thing we aren't skimping on, though, is mining equipment. We know there'll be minerals in the ground, and we have to be able to get to them. We'll need them. So, we're sending a lot of mining equipment, explosives, and miners. Some of the crucial people that get to go are miners. "I'm a hard rock miner. I walk through rock." That's what they say. And it's true. It can be raining a hurricane out in the open, and they're still working far underground. It doesn't bother them.

24

JOURNAL
The First Arcasians

The lack of electricity is aggravating! We spent the whole day without power today. Nobody could get any work done. Sure, we talked about plans, but couldn't document anything. I've told my team to print out everything they have. The power's going to get worse as time goes on. We can't have our work crippled by not being able to get at something on a computer.

My last journal entry mentioned miners, and they're going to be important. They have skills that'll help in a lot of areas. Aside from mining, they can help clear and level surface areas. They can also make caves for shelter and workspaces. We'll be able to get some shelters and building materials to Arcas, but don't know what the weather will be like. If there are intense storms, the shelters may not be enough.

Manmade caves are a backup plan, though. The first plan for shelter is monolithic domes. They're very durable, and we don't have to send all of the materials. The concrete for them comes from cement mix, plus water, sand, and rock. We may not be able to find the ingredients for cement on Arcas, but water, sand, and gravel will be plentiful. It'll just be lying around ready to be collected. So, it's going to take a lot of fuel to send cement powder, but it's what's needed. Along with the powder mix, there'll be inflatable forms to send. They get blown up first, concrete is put on to harden, and the form is deflated to be used for another dome. The colonists will be able to make a lot of strong domes that'll withstand storms in a short amount of time.

––––––––––––––––––

Back to the miners, though. We're going to send a heck of a lot of explosives to Arcas for them. That worries me. Moving that much explosives could be tricky. What if we pack them all into one capsule and something explodes? Then they're all gone. What if we split them up and pack them amongst all of the capsules with other supplies, and some explode? Then we lose lots of other supplies we need. We've decided the risk of packing capsules full of explosives is worth taking. It isn't just going to be one capsule, however. There'll be a lot of capsules with a lot of materials.

I figure we'll be using explosives at an amazing rate on Arcas at the beginning. After talking about it at work, another skillset we decided we need is chemists and chemical manufacturers. After all, we need to have people who can make more explosives. And, of course, all of their equipment. More equipment.

I feel like I keep repeating that point at work. Every time I say something about a type of skill we'll need on Arcas, I say we'll need the equipment and machines they use. But, that's how it is. For every type of work, they'll need their tools. It all has to be taken.

I've written about miners and manufacturers, but the most important persons we're going to need on Arcas is farmers. There's a huge industry around producing food here on Earth that won't be on Arcas when we get there. Many parts of our food production process are invisible to me. I've seen news articles about farms when there's some food problem, but barely know where the food at the grocery store comes from these days.

The people who go to Arcas will need a lot of food. The fact that they'll be heavier means the exertion of normal living will cause them to burn more calories. Part of the supplies the government's been stockpiling on the Moon is food, mostly freeze-dried stuff and military MREs. The MREs will be edible for years, but aren't as tasty as fresh food. The colonists will need to be able to grow food as soon as possible, and a lot of it.

The government talks about doing interviews for miners, workers, etc. Every time they bring this up, I tell them they need to talk to them at their homes and look in the back yard. They need to look for gardens and landscaping boxes. Whomever is picked for jobs other than farming, we should consider how skilled they are at being home gardeners. Everybody's going to need to be at least three levels deep in skills for Arcas. Gardening is the closest to farming and is the most important secondary skill anyone can have. Other things like woodworking, welding, weaving, sewing, cooking, and baking are needed, but gardening is most important. You can always eat raw food, but you have to have the food first. Everyone's going to have to be able to contribute in multiple ways and pitch in where needed. Canning foods, smoking meats, and tanning hides. God, there are so many skills we have to remember to teach people.

I also tell the interviewers a close second to look for is past military service. Any type of participation in organized groups will work, really, as long as they've had to be part of a team and work together for the good of the group. Military people will know that mindset, even if they've been out for a while. On the other hand, college professors and doctors not so much. A lot of them act like they're the leaders of their own kingdoms. That's not what will help the first Arcasians survive. They need to be able to cooperate with each other.

Even though we'll be sending people with farming skills, there won't be good dirt on Arcas for farming, but Briar Patch has worked on that, too. Hydroponics, air farming, all kinds of different techniques. They worked over the years on the science for this whole thing while we get to do the practical legwork. God, there's so much advancement that's happened that's being applied to this transfer. I never suspected it was going on. Anyway, we need farmers to grow food using the techniques developed for scarce soils. Eventually, there'll be some dirt for farming in the ground. We need farmers who can do it all.

25

JOURNAL
Skills

The first set of people have been selected to go to Arcas and are arriving here for orientation and training. After they get a detailed briefing on Arcas, we're introducing them to as many manual skills as possible. With less than six months before the first pass of Arcas and less than a year before they'll be going there themselves, there's a lot for them to learn in a short amount of time. They're being fast tracked into advanced survival training, but are also learning about trade skills. The only skills that are going to be on Arcas are the ones they take with them. It's not like they can call someone from Earth for an emergency plumbing repair on a Sunday night. Earth will be far away and help will be nonexistent.

It's hard to list all of the skills they're being taught. They're learning carpentry, masonry, foundry skills, plumbing, electrical, mining, farming, sewing, baking, cooking, butchering, drafting, architecture, papermaking, medicine, herbology, chemistry, etc. As much as we can teach. Everyone's being exposed to the full gamut, no matter who they are or what they've done in the past. It's a pretty grueling schedule of six-hour crash course sessions followed by more individualized training. It's difficult for them, but nobody's giving up. If you give up, then you're out of the program, which means you'll be staying on Earth and giving up your life. None of them want that.

We realize the group isn't going to be able to absorb all of the knowledge across all of the skills we're exposing them to. That's why we're also sending skill manuals. The most essential and basic skills are going to be in booklet form so there's an easily accessible hard copy, but everything is going to be sent on digital media so we can send it all. We're collecting and digitizing every "how to" book and video we can find. Luckily, the internet is full of all kinds of how-to videos.

An overarching theme to the training is stressing the importance of teaching the future generations how to use computers to get at all of the knowledge we've developed. We're not fooling ourselves in this area. There aren't going to be enough people to possibly know as much as humanity knows now, and there's going to be a long dip in computer usage as the people establish a society. The Arcasians are going to have their hands full with basic survival for years and aren't going to be able to think about things as complex as producing webcasts. It's essential we don't forget how to use the computers and lose all of the progress humanity has made. The future Arcasians need to know how to get at the information they'll have, even if they don't understand it at the time.

26
JOURNAL
Chickens

I had a panic attack at work today over chickens. Of all the stupid things to worry about, it was chickens. I know my stress level's really high, but didn't know something like thinking about chickens would set me off. It started with my vision getting little sparkling flashes as I stared at the wall. Then it started closing into a funnel shape and tunnel vision. I was sweating and nauseous, had the chills, and started hyperventilating. I bent over and sat in my chair with my head between my knees and the garbage can between my feet in case I threw up. It was ten minutes before I felt good enough to sit up. I may be able to laugh about this in the future, but not now.

It all started because chickens will be sent to Arcas, and they seem so fragile and, I don't know, breakable. It feels like a chicken is a balloon that can suddenly pop with an explosion of feathers. Like any minor scare will cause it to grasp its chest and die of a heart attack on the spot.

Chickens are essential, though. They're going to be useful for food and for manure. They lay eggs almost every day, and eggs are a very useful food. Eggs are full of good protein and cholesterol to power the hardworking Arcasians. They can be hard-boiled and taken anywhere for an easy meal. They're also ingredients in many other foods. And chicken poop is a very useful fertilizer. It's very balanced, but has a lot of nitrogen so it's very "hot". It has to be composted or it'll burn out whatever you put it on.

The frailty of chickens worries me. Arcas's gravity is one and a half times what we have, and chickens are so small. They can't fly so that's not a big deal, but I was worried they won't be able to stand up, and their eggs will break.

After I calmed down, I got the team together to talk it over. They helped me feel better. We got some eggs, weighed our computer manuals, and stacked them onto the eggs to make sure they wouldn't break. It wasn't an extremely controlled experiment, but I hope NASA would be proud of our ingenuity under the circumstances. We decided after placing the fifth manual chicken eggs are strong enough they won't break in the Arcas gravity. Also, since chickens are small, we reasoned they'll be okay because they have less weight for their muscles to carry. Kind of like how little kids seem like they can run forever because they weigh less. Adults aren't as good at running because they weigh more.

Just to be safe, we're going to do something that sounded ridiculous when it was first brought up. We're going to fit the chickens with weight vests and let them walk around a little heavier until transfer time. We're all doing it, so why not the chickens? By the time they go to Arcas, their drumsticks are going to be bulked up like a Ms. Universe contestant.

Sarah from our team went out and found a group of seamstresses to work on custom chicken vests. After they stopped laughing about the job we explained to them, they talked a mile a minute about plans and cut patterns. I didn't understand most of the conversation. As they got more excited about the idea, they talked about making the outfits with different fabric patterns and colors to customize each chicken. Maybe they could sew small ties on the outfits, and we could initiate them as honorary Briar Patch Group members. I bet they end up being more stylish than I am. Jeez, I'm going to have to step up my work clothes so I'm not outclassed by chickens.

Tomorrow afternoon, I'm going to watch someone try to hold a chicken while they measure it for a "tuxedo". Although I can't say anything, I secretly hope it gets loose, and I get to watch them chase it around the room while I imagine lively banjo music in my head. That would give us all a much-needed laugh.

All of the animals we decide to take will need similar consideration. Goats with ankle weights. Birds flying with weights. I knew I should have bought stock in weight companies. Except for the fact it'd be worthless.

Oh, good God, I just thought of something else. We have to take worms. I need to add that to the list. Nobody's thought of worms yet. They're great for composting and churning through soils. And bugs. We need bugs. Bugs do a lot of the first step of composting. They break up materials, eat food scraps, and poop out their own tiny manure. Yep, we'll need to take bugs. Maybe we won't outfit the bugs and worms with weights, though.

27
JOURNAL
The President Speaks Again

Things are getting more tense. Arcas is visible and will be making its first pass in a couple of months. It's a bright dot in the sky, and everyone knows where it is. I could ask anybody over the age of six, and they'd be able to point it out. There's no need for that, though. I know exactly where Arcas is and how much time we have left.

Supplies are getting scarcer in stores. Before we could really see Arcas, things were doing okay. Now we can see it, and people are getting depressed. They aren't working as much anymore, and manufacturing has slowed down. Granted, Jenny and I don't need anything like new towels or an accent chair, but it hurts when the shelves in the grocery store aren't as filled as they once were. The cleaning supplies and paper products are scarce. Before long, it's going to get harder to find food.

I was happy when the President decided to speak to the nation again. Of course, he talked about Arcas in his State of the Union a few months ago, but that didn't exactly address people in the country directly. I thought he gave a good speech. It wasn't the best I've ever heard, but my mental condition isn't the same as it's been, either, so I'm not in the best position to judge it.

"My fellow Americans. It was about this time last year when I stood in front of you and gave you some grave news. I'm not ashamed to tell you that was one of the worst days of my life, but I was elected to serve you in the bad times as well as the good. Since then, I hope there have been good times in your lives. The First Lady and I are happy to admit to you the joy we felt as we watched our son graduate from college recently. Given the circumstances, we're proud of his decision to finish the education he started. We hope you've had such moments, too.

"As time has passed this year, the business of the country has continued. You're in my thoughts every day and in every decision I make. This is an unprecedented situation, and we are demonstrating patience, understanding, and compassion with each other.

"The work on ships to transfer some Americans to Arcas is progressing well. Progress is also being made toward terraforming the planet for its first inhabitants. It hasn't had an atmosphere, or plant and animal life, and that needs to be conditioned and introduced as much as possible before people arrive. Everything is proceeding on schedule, and all of the pieces will be in place when they're needed.

"This process is not without its own pain points, though. It has put a strain on some of the governmental resources, but we're making adjustments to compensate for services that have suffered. The country's security is of paramount importance.

"During last year's rioting, the army was deployed to safeguard and escort commerce around the country. As our courageous troops have come home from overseas, they've been included in this effort and have been redeployed to other vital areas.

"Despite our best efforts, we're beginning to see supply shortages in some places. I've been meeting with heads of companies and am encouraging them to continue business as usual to the fullest extent possible. To that end, I also want to encourage each of you to continue your lives with as little disruption as you can. For our country's stability, it's important to keep ourselves occupied and heartened.

"I implore you to be kind to your fellow Americans. Be helpful. Perform a random act of kindness for a neighbor. Enjoy the time we have with each other and try to notice the small joys that surround us every day.

"My fellow Americans, I love you, and I love this country. We will have more challenges, but must also remember to celebrate our victories over our adversities. I wish you joy as we continue on this journey together. God bless you. God bless your families. And God bless the United States of America."

28
THREE QUEENS
Stephanie's Spring

Stephanie looked at the laundry piled in front of her. Steve, the kids, and she didn't have a lot of clothes, but there always seemed to be a big pile to wash. She didn't buy clothes for herself unless something of hers wore out because Steve would notice and yell at her about spending money on it. The kids had more outfits because Stephanie was able to get old things at yard sales if she looked around carefully. Sometimes she could bargain for two pieces for fifty cents rather than one.

One of Steve's striped work shirts with his embroidered "Steve" name patch sat on top of the pile. Underneath was Stephanie's shirt with spots of dried blood from the bloody nose she got last night when Steve hit her. *Why does the President have to speak?* she thought when she was closing the door to the childrens' room before his speech. *Any talk about Arcas sets Steve off. The President should come here personally to take the beating, and I'll go to sleep in his warm bed.*

Stephanie snatched her shirt from the pile and worked on the stain. She wet it and scrubbed the fabric back and forth between her hands before loading it into the washer. She was careful to keep the side of her face concealed from the other people at the laundromat and had picked a spot where she could keep her head turned away so they couldn't see the uneven redness on her left cheek. All of the clothes went into one load to save money on the number of washes she did.

Stephanie and Steve hadn't had white sheets on their bed in years. All of her white undergarments had a bluish-grey tint from many washings with other colors. The edges were frayed from tumbling around with tough denim jean material. Having something bright white might have briefly lifted her spirits, but then she would pull the dulled material out of its first wash and her spirit would dull as quickly as the fabric. What was the point of trying to have a bright spot in your life when it would just darken and become ragged in a little while?

She counted out the coins for the washing machine and dryer one more time to make sure she had brought enough for both today. Once, a long time ago, she had dropped a coin when the baby she was holding suddenly jerked. It bounced, flipped perfectly into the thin gap between the washing machines, and rattled as it slid to the floor. Every time she went to the laundromat afterwards she remembered the feeling of desperation at having to dip into the grocery money to pay for a machine, and she carefully held each coin as she counted them from one pile to another. She never wanted to hear that metallic clank again.

29

THREE QUEENS
Susan's Spring

Susan looked at the laundry piled in front of her. The pile was large, but that was normal. *How on Earth do we wear so many clothes?* she thought. She mused about that. *How on Earth? That's funny.* She never realized before how often she used the phrase, "How on Earth." As she thought about it, she smiled sadly. *The people on Arcas will have to come up with a new phrase in the future.*

The kids' clothes were on top of the pile because she had emptied those baskets onto the bed after hers. The jeans had their usual grass stained knees and dirtier parts on the thighs where the boys wiped their hands. *I'm glad they're still getting out to play and have some fun.* She inspected the jeans for ripped knees. Whenever the knees tore on the kids' jeans, she would replace them with a fresh pair and turn the old pair into cut-off shorts.

As she sorted the clothes and towels into piles by color and type of fabric, her mind wandered to the President's speech. *He said something about acts of kindness. That would be nice. Our family is so blessed. We can do something nice for someone else. It'll be a good example for the children, too.* As she continued to sort, she absently thought of different people she knew and what would be helpful to them.

The clothes piles moved through the steps of bedroom to clothes basket, clothes basket to dirty pile, dirty pile to washer, washer to dryer, dryer to folding table, folding table to clothes basket, and clothes basket to bedroom. Susan had happily gone through the process like an orchestrated ballet every week for nearly as long as she could remember. For her, it was meditative, and it was a pleasure to do for her family. She used the time to think about her family and friends. As she went about the process, she sometimes wondered if the cycle was one of God's ways of letting her glimpse His grace. She would never presume to equate her weekly laundry to His infiniteness and wisdom, but wondered if its continuous nature would one day help her fathom His limitlessness when she eventually stood in His presence.

30
THREE QUEENS
Karen's Spring

Karen looked at the laundry piled in front of her. It wasn't overly large, but it needed to be done. She did her washing every couple of weeks after she accumulated enough for a full load. Each load happened individually because there might not be a full load of colors when the whites were ready, or whites when the towels and sheets needed washing. Laundry used a lot of clean water which needed to be conserved, and soap that took time to break down in the environment.

Today's laundry was a mass of rags with an assortment of Dodger's sleeping blankets from around the house. Dodger's fur wove into the old blankets as he twisted back and forth on his back on them to scratch an itch. The rags were mostly towels Karen used to dry Dodger when she gave him a bath. They smelled like a musty, wet dog who had enjoyed his bath immensely.

Karen was glad for the warmer weather they were having. She would hang her laundry outside to dry, even in the winter, but it was nice when she took it inside with a summery smell from drying on a warm day rather than a cold crispness from freeze drying in the dry wintry air. *I hope this weather soothes the rioters*, she thought. It made Karen sad they weren't showing respect to Mother Earth and were being so destructive. She had noticed the increased army turnout the President talked about the night before. She hoped there could be a better solution than this form of martial law.

31

JOURNAL
Kepler's Laws of Planetary Motion

I thought I'd take this journal entry to write down Kepler's laws of planetary motion. We've talked about them enough at work trying to make sense of our disbelief of how Arcas is actually happening. Johannes Kepler worked with Tycho Brahe and came up with three laws of planetary motion. Brahe spent his nights taking precise measurements of the planets, and Kepler deciphered them into the laws of how the planets move. As I said, we talk about them at work, and draw lots of orbit pictures on the white board, to try to wrap our heads around each step Arcas will be taking. The odds of it being on this exact path rather than one that shoots by Earth or crashes into it are practically unfathomable to us.

Number one. Planets move in an elliptical orbit. Everyone looks at the drawings of the solar system and thinks the planets make circles around the Sun, but they're actually ellipses. A circle has one focal point, the center, while an ellipse has two. In the case of the planets, the two foci of their ellipses are close together so the orbit looks nearly circular.

Number two. Planets sweep out equal areas of the ellipse as measured from the Sun in the same amount of time. It took us a while to wrap our heads around this law. I know I learned it in high school physics, but forgot it. It means the planets travel slightly faster when they're closer to the Sun and slightly slower when they're away from the Sun. Not a big deal since the orbits are nearly circular.

Number three is more of a doozy, and it's all mathematical. The square of the orbital period of a planet is directly proportional to the cube of the semi-major axis of its orbit. That gobbledygook doesn't mean much to us, but it's very important. It's the equation of a planet's orbit and how long it takes to go around the Sun. The math of it is part of why they know Arcas is going to be in an orbit around the Sun when this is all over.

We also talked a lot at work early on about how we were amazed nobody's noticed Arcas before now. Of course the Briar Patch Group has influenced where astronomers were looking, but it's also not coming at us from the same plane as the other planets. If it were, people might have found Arcas while looking at them.

Arcas is a bit askew to the planet orbits. There's complicated physics involved that is way over my head, but essentially it's coming "up" at us from the south to the north. Since there's no other gravity affecting it, it's moving in a straight line right now. When it passes by the first time, the path it's on is going to be bent by the Earth. It's going to be captured in the Sun's gravity and swing around it to come back past us in six months. At that point, it's going to get another tug of gravity from the Earth that'll bend it into an elliptical orbit around the Sun as we get flung out of our orbit. The square of its orbital period will be directly proportional to the cube of the semi-major axis of its orbit. What could be simpler than that?

32
JOURNAL
Terraforming

With Arcas coming closer and growing larger in the sky, we can finally see the place we're shooting for. It's still just a small spot in the sky, but it has universal importance to us. It's scary to think that our only hope is to make it hospitable for human life. Every day it feels overwhelming to be in charge of something so big. We deal with disasters on large scales, but not planetary scales.

To say terraforming is going to be difficult is an understatement. It's a huge problem because it's always been theoretical, and all of the theoretical scenarios have been in places that have dirt and water already. Terraforming isn't as easy as the movies make it sound. In an ideal situation, it would take years, even centuries, to kick start a stable planetary ecosystem. We have a little over a year to do a project the size of a planet, and it's never been done before.

One thing in our favor is Arcas will have water by the time we're going to be terraforming. The surface ice will melt in a little while as it gets closer to the Sun. It definitely won't have dirt for plants, though. It has its regolith dust, but not rich, organic dirt. Since there's never been anything living there, there's no organic matter whatsoever for soil.

Everything organic at the start will have to come from Earth or be made by the plants we send early on.

Arcas will have water, which is good. Everyone says there'll be an atmosphere, although they aren't exactly sure what its composition will be. It could be nitrogen, it could be oxygen, carbon dioxide, methane, sulfur. Who knows? It'll have some of all of them, but we don't know the absolute amount of atmosphere or the portions of each type of gas in it.

Since there's going to be water, our first step will be introducing cyanobacteria into it. In other words blue-green algae. We'll send other types of algae and microbes, too, to have some variety, but the majority will be blue-green. It's an excellent photosynthesizer and produces oxygen at a high rate. As soon as Arcas is in the habitable zone, we'll start sending capsules loaded with it. We're making little cages for it to live in and around called apartments. When it gets into the water, we don't want the algae to just float away. If it does, I doubt it'd survive. There wouldn't be any nutrients for it. Thus, the apartments. The algae will be loaded onto a mesh framework with a supply of nutrients to help it grow and stay together. It'll be at least a year's worth of nutrients for a colony ten times the size of what we're sending so it can get a good start.

The capsules with the apartments are going to be sent every ten days as much as we can. The rocket builders are working on assembly lines around the clock to build the huge number we need. Since each launch needs its own trajectory calculations, the astrophysicists are keeping busy with those calculations. Unlike the stockpiles that have been going to the Moon, these capsules will have to be heated so the algae doesn't die in space. We're thinking of adding radioactive elements for heat. Might as well have the algae take some reactor fuel for the nuclear power when they go, but it's going to be a balance between heating them and killing them with radiation.

Other than this, there isn't much more to the plan for the atmosphere. We're doing what we can and have to cross our fingers for luck. The algae is going to have eight months to crank out as much oxygen as it can. It isn't as long as we'd like, but we can't make Arcas move slower. The apartments are going to float in whatever water they land in. Nothing's going to be able to float in the air, and nothing's going to be able to survive on the land until we have a better idea what it looks like and where it is relative to oceans. The best way we figured to have the greatest dispersion of the algae is for them to drift on water.

33
JOURNAL
Public Paranoia

Sometimes I just can't believe people. A new wave of public paranoia has started. They've started freaking out about aliens and getting eggs in their brains, or some nonsense like that. Like they're even going to be on Arcas for that! We used to post things like this on the bulletin board in the break room and took turns making up fake ones to see if anyone could tell the difference. It just isn't fun anymore because the real-life topics are stranger than anything we ever came up with.

It seems like someone watched a few too many alien horror movies and has taken them too seriously. The latest "news" wave going around is Arcas will have eggs from an alien species. The story goes like this: as soon as the planet is warm again, the eggs will hatch and the aliens will overrun any humans who land there. It's a load of cow manure, of course, but you can't stop that kind of rumor after it starts. The crowds and the news organizations will talk about it even after it's been debunked.

Most rational people will listen to reason. The planet has been in the emptiness of space, and nothing has ever lived on it. It wouldn't be logical for aliens to land on it and leave eggs, or anything else. The problem is the rumor-mongers will question how you can know for sure it isn't the case. Eventually someone will answer by saying something like, "There's no way to know with absolute certainty, but the likelihood of anything like that is incredibly low." That's all they'll need to justify their position and go on the attack to keep the hysteria going. They'll say, "So you're saying it's possible," and twist the other person's clear explanation into knots.

Another rumor that went around before the alien eggs is Arcas will have alien viruses that will wipe out the people who land. Sort of a *War of the Worlds* story theory. That's ridiculous for the same reason. Although it's true we wouldn't have any immunity to Arcasian germs, there simply aren't any. The planet has never had conditions that would spawn self-replicating complex organic molecules. It just can't have happened.

34
JOURNAL
Hiding Out

I had to drive a long way to get home today. The army had the main highway closed off, and I had to take neighborhood streets to get home. That was kind of scary because some of the neighborhoods have been looted pretty badly. Our work time in the office is shorter now because we leave work while it's still light so we can get home before dark. Since it took longer this afternoon, it was nearly dark when I got home. I was starting to get worried. If you're in the wrong place after sunset, you can be in real trouble.

The rioting has started again. Our house was spared during the first round, but it's getting closer each night. Jenny's still mad at me. I'm kicked out of the bedroom going on seven months, but we've reached the point where we can talk about the situation now.

We're fortunate that Max's school year ended last month. He rode his bike to school, and it would be too dangerous for him now. Only about half of the teachers were showing up toward the end of the semester. It had become more of a place for the kids to go, be with their friends, and play. People are realizing the everyday life we knew isn't going to mean anything in less than two years so they've started giving up on it.

Jenny and I have been talking about what we want to do to stay safe. She wants to go to her parents' place farther outside of the city while I want us to stay here. Regardless of where we are and what other people are doing, I still have to go to work. If we're farther away, it means it'll take me longer to get to work, and it would take longer to get home if anything unexpected happened.

We're going to stay here for now, but it gets more tense each day. We're going to move into the shelter and hide out there. It has room for a lot of supplies and is hidden. I restocked the shelves with canned goods when the rioting started after the President's first speech about Arcas. I'm also going to stop taking care of the lawn and make a mess of the front of the house to camouflage it. It's not like we'll need a nice looking property when this is over in a couple of years. There's no resale value when nobody's going to be looking to buy. We want it to look like it's been ransacked already so people will leave it alone. They go after anything unbroken first so I'll start by breaking all the windows. That sucks. I like my windows.

Max'll get a kick out of helping me trash the place. We'll do it quietly, aside from the sound of shattering glass, and slowly so we don't alert the neighbors. Maybe we'll get lucky and a "gentle" mob will pass by and help us out.

35
JOURNAL
By Myself

That didn't last long. Jenny left today. She took Max and went to her parents' house. The riots came through here two days ago and scared the hell out of her even though we were safe in the shelter. Nobody could find us in there, but it was too much for Jenny to take. She thinks it's too dangerous to stay here now.

Suffice it to say we had a huge fight about it last night, and she'd had enough. There was nothing I could do to convince her to stay. I can't leave, though. Jenny's parents live too far away for me to commute to work, and I <u>have</u> to keep going to work. The work we're doing is helping the human race survive. How could I abandon that? How could I leave such an important task up to someone else?

On the bright side, the house looks more abandoned now. I can't believe I'm trying to find a bright side in all of this. The shelter is holding up nicely. I've been restocking the food we were eating so we could use it as long as possible. I guess it's still denial on my part to do that. It's not like a few days will matter either way once the Earth has gotten its "fling" from Arcas, but it gives me something to do.

I don't know what I'll do with my time without Jenny and Max here.

Maybe I'll finally read the *Odyssey*. I've always wanted to, but have never been motivated enough to tackle it in the past. Right now, an epic poem about a sailor beset by impossible task after impossible task seems apropos. Odysseus was trying to get himself and his crew home from the war, and I'm trying to get a crew to a new home. Okay, it's a bit of a stretch to compare my life to Homer's *Odyssey*, but I hope I can be forgiven for being a little dramatic, my wife and kid just left me.

36
JOURNAL
Back Together

Good news! The family's back together again. I mentioned at work Jenny and Max had moved out. It turns out we weren't the only family being torn apart by safety concerns. FEMA decided it would be best to move everyone working on the Arcas project to some secure housing. They explained how we'd be able to work better without the worry of our loved ones being somewhere else. I think they're right. My whole team is moving with their families.

I told Jenny the good news, but she didn't take it as positively. She almost didn't come. She's an only child and is worried about her parents. Like any good parents watching out for their child, however, they convinced her to take Max and go. Their place is far enough away from the city it hasn't had any trouble.

We moved into a small apartment in the warehouse district. It's an abandoned motel complex. The building is two stories tall with room doors along the outside. It has stairways at either end of the outside hallway and a set in the middle. We have the equivalent of two motel rooms with an adjoining door between them. They built an extra wall in each to divide the rooms into more spaces, but they're really small. The whole facility has a new chain link fence, complete with guards on patrol.

We've been here a few days, and I've given our "apartment" some thought. Our living space is large enough we could fit Jenny's parents with us. It would be pretty uncomfortable to cram five of us into such a small space, but we could do it for the safety and sanity factor. Even though they live farther out of the city, it'll be much safer here. I can tell Jenny's been thinking about it, too.

I'm going to give us another week to settle in and see how we adjust into the space before we make any decisions. FEMA wouldn't approve of more people moving in, but maybe Jenny's parents could come over for a "housewarming" and just quietly not leave. We'll have to go over some excuses they can give if people start noticing them around more. The door leading directly outside isn't going to help. Jenny can always say they came to help her with Max.

37

JOURNAL
What Do You Mean, Arcas Approaching?

We can finally say Arcas is here. It's been visible in the sky for a long time, but we were able to ignore it. We can't anymore as it grows bigger and spookier each day. Right now, it appears the same size as the Moon and brighter in a way, but it isn't blotchy white like the Moon. It's dark grey with blue water areas. We were all pleased when we could see water and realized there's enough to make oceans. The terraforming algae will have a lot of room to float.

Because it looks the same size as the Moon and accounting for its size, its distance from Earth right now is about seven times the distance to the Moon. It's going to get bigger for a while and then will start to recede.

In general, people have been cranky for a while, but having it appear like a second moon has made people more on edge because it's always there. There's a noticeable amount of stress in every situation. If you say "Hi" to someone on the street, you don't know what's going to happen. They might say "Hi" back, they might grumble something at you, or they might start crying. It's hard to tell how anyone will react. As I said, it's hard to ignore the reality anymore.

Arcas has been in the "habitable zone" of the solar system for a while. Almost everyone with any kind of telescope has been looking at it. We can see the frozen materials on its surface have melted. As predicted, there are some oceans, and there is an atmosphere. The good news is there's a lot of carbon dioxide. The algae will work on converting it to oxygen. Immense terraforming issue step one, check.

We're sending the algae apartments to Arcas now. There're being aimed at every body of water we can find. The effort uses a lot of rocket fuel because Arcas is still far away, but we have to do it. We thought about trying to add other supplies in the nooks and crannies of the rockets, but gave that idea up. We can't put in anything like a box of nails or a pair of pliers because they'd sink in the water. They'd never be recovered. And, sending anything like a little bit of fertilizer or organic material isn't worth the fuel cost. It would cost a lot of fuel to get some small amount of nutrients there that aren't intended for the algae. Those things would completely disperse in the water as if it wasn't even sent. We don't have to worry about guiding the capsules too much or bringing any back to Earth so that saves a little of the fuel load.

On a whim, I managed to sneak one of Max's toy sailboats into a capsule. Alan Shepard got to hit a golf ball on the Moon. We get to be the first people to play with a toy on Arcas. I chuckle every time I imagine this little sailboat bobbing up and down on the Arcas ocean. I see it smiling, if it could, since it has the whole place to itself.

In a little while, we'll send a different type of apartment that holds ants and food for them. Since there's a layer of regolith on Arcas, we want the ants to start breaking it up and moving it around. They'll tunnel into it which will make some space for air to penetrate. They'll be able to break up some of the rock, too. They can find weaker spots to chip away and burrow into the surface. We hope that'll help release some gases trapped in the dust and start it on its way to being farmable. Or maybe just gardenable on a small scale.

Similarly, we're going to start sending the first land plants. We have to try getting some solidity into the regolith so it doesn't blow away like a dustbowl in whatever type of wind Arcas has. We're going to send seed of many different types of plants balled up in packs with starter nutrients: grasses, grains, wildflowers, shrubs, and trees. I don't like it, but we'll also be sending dandelions. Those things are the bane of my summer lawn! They have their long tap root that makes them so hard to get rid of. Anyway, the plants will get the carbon and oxygen they need from the air and will use photosynthesis to make their food, and they'll send their roots into any slight cracks in the ground to get the minerals they need to grow. We've seen a few clouds and assume there's some kind of precipitation going on, but haven't confirmed it yet. Even though the clouds are light and wispy, it's a good sign. If there are clouds, there should be precipitation that can filter into the surface for plants to get with their roots.

All of the non-algae capsules are being targeted to a smaller area we've identified where we want to establish our colony. The entire surface of the planet is so vast we can't try to seed it all. We have to focus the resources we have on establishing patches of vegetation. The place selected is near the shore of an ocean, which will provide another option for food in the long run after fish and other ocean dwellers become established.

There's such a long list of plants we're sending to try to grow. The best would have been bamboo because it grows much quicker than other plants, but it doesn't start from seed very easily. We're going to take the chance and send a small amount of bamboo grafts, but are mostly sending seeds of other types of plants. We're going to send seaweed to the ocean near the colony area, too. It may float around, but we're hoping some will anchor itself nearby. These are bases of the ecosystem we're trying to introduce, and all of it has to be sent from here. Everything needed to support the animals, birds, reptiles, insects, etc. that come later has to be sent early so it can become established.

About a month after we start sending the seeds, we're going to send honey bees. The plants need pollinators or they won't be able to produce new seeds. The bees can build their own houses so we don't have to send a lot of supporting materials for them. With luck, there'll be some yummy honey waiting for the colonizers when they arrive.

38

THE ASTRONAUTS
Quarter for Your Thoughts

Beckson had three months left on the Moon. Three more shipments, and he would be going home to begin the next segment of his mission. Back on Earth, he knew he'd rotate into the shifts on the CAPCOM desk after his body recovered from its extended period of reduced gravity to monitor and communicate with the Moon crew. Aside from Johnson, the former Moon astronauts who shared the CAPCOM shifts were the only people he had talked to in a very long time. They'd been indispensable when he first arrived on the Moon as they calmly gave advice about living on the Moon and explanations about the facility. Despite his training, Beckson knew nobody could be completely prepared to live on the Moon. He had been grateful for the knowledge they imparted in a friendly manner and for the occasional joke they told.

He tucked away a mental note to walk when he got back rather than try to get around by bounding like on the Moon. It felt like a long time since he had walked anywhere. If he tried bounding on Earth, he'd fall flat on his face. Although he was looking forward to being back on Earth, he wasn't thrilled about being on a doomed planet. With his space experience and Moon service, he hoped they would pick him to go to

Arcas.

His replacement, Peterson, was coming with the next shipment along with two more astronauts to get the supplies ready for launch to Arcas. Beckson knew Peterson from their training. He was a good man. He and Johnson would finish the mission together. Beckson didn't know the other two astronauts, though. He didn't even know their names. He had seen them while they were training, but they had a different mission which involved different training.

Six years of shipments were ready. Canisters were stacked neatly in rows in the Maksutov crater, chosen for its level surface. Rows of launch ships were lined up opposite the canisters, and fuel pods were dispersed across other locations. Everything was prepared to begin transferring the supplies to Arcas after it captured the Moon in an orbit. Johnson, Peterson, and the other two astronauts wouldn't have long to wait before that part of the mission started.

39
JOURNAL
Crowded House

Jenny's parents are moved in now. It's still summer and hot, but we're keeping the windows open to stay cooler. Even fewer people are showing up for their jobs these days, and the electric company is feeling the strain of it. There are rolling blackouts around the city during most days. We aren't able to run electric fans to have some air movement in our apartment, but we hooked up something we can crank by hand. We're never quite sure if we'll be able to use the stove and oven to cook supper. Sometimes all the neighbors cook their meals on an old charcoal grill we salvaged.

Max has a few friends that he goes outside to play with. Like everyone who doesn't have to venture out of the compound to work, they stay inside the fence all the time. It isn't safe to go out, even during the day. You never know who's prowling around outside the fence, and how hungry or desperate they are. We do our best to keep safe.

It's going well with Jenny's parents. Well, it's going as well as it can when you live with your elderly in-laws. I think some people suspect they're living with us, but nobody's complaining because everyone's doing it. It seems like a lot of people had their own "housewarming" for relatives. The building has gotten very crowded, but everyone is looking the other way. Nobody wants to turn out their neighbor's family and then have their own family evicted. On the plus side, Max is spending time getting to know his grandparents. That's a good thing. Mine are gone so these are the only ones he'll know.

Jenny's mom was a school teacher and is homeschooling a lot of the kids in the complex. Even though it's summer vacation time, we're trying to keep them busy so they'll be distracted from the thought of Arcas coming. I don't think they're doing any strenuous teaching, but are keeping the kids occupied. That's one of the reasons nobody's ratting us out. Jenny's mom is working and providing a service to the whole community. She's recruited some of the other "housewarming" grandmas to help, and they've split the kids into age groups to make it easier. Honestly, it's also keeping the grandmas busy and distracted from the big planet in the sky.

Having five of us living in our small apartment isn't easy. Max sleeps in the bedroom with us, and Jenny's parents have the second bedroom. We took out the single bed that was in there and moved in a queen bed for them. There's not much open floor space in their room, but they have a comfortable place to sleep. We have a blow up mattress in our bedroom for Max. He's tolerating it well enough.

––––––––––––––––––

In other news, we've moved our work offices inside the compound, too. We probably should have done this sooner, but we've had other things on our minds. The world is getting too dangerous to have the team try to commute to the office. Moving into the compound makes good sense because everyone lives here anyway. Not to mention gas is in short supply. It won't be long before we won't be able to drive at all.

The compound's size is being expanded to accommodate more working space and space for the colonists. More army personnel will be arriving to increase the security. With so many people to protect, the compound's basically turned into a small army base.

The groups selected by the government have been here and training for a while. We've been very happy with their progress. They've been very disciplined and have given great feedback on the program. They're working closely with their instructors to design class modules for the lottery colonists. They've learned, will have some time to practice, and then will teach the new recruits. The whole training program will be better the second time through since the first group is going to be involved in the training.

Colonists picked by lottery will come after it happens. They'll live and train in the newer facilities. I wonder what their impression will be when they get here. Many of them will have been out of school for a long time. The change of pace of going back to a learning environment may be a bit of a shock.

40
JOURNAL
Come and Gone

Well, that sucked. Arcas made its first pass by the Earth. I missed a lot of journaling time because things were very hectic at work. We had to pause all of our Arcas planning and switch to triaging disasters. New disasters were happening on a daily basis. We'd work during the day at the building (we have a separate building in the housing complex) to coordinate disaster crew efforts and would meet informally for several hours afterwards to analyze the day. We all took turns staying at the building overnight to answer new calls from across the country and prepare a briefing for the next morning. Arcas is still affecting things, but the worst is over. The worst. How can I even say that? Millions of people have died. Whole cities have been wiped out. The geography of some places has been drastically altered.

Saying it was rough would be like saying, shit, I don't know what. "Biblical" is about the only word that comes to mind. It began like a gigantic version of Death by a Thousand Paper Cuts where each tiny cut stings a little at the beginning, but the pain builds up and gets worse and worse in anticipation of the next cut. That was how it was at the beginning. It was slow, but unrelenting, and it grew. Eventually, the scale was immense. The devastation was horrific for the two months Arcas was closest to the Earth.

In addition to the physical devastation, there was incredible mental devastation among the public. We saw destruction of the kind never witnessed by humans. Every time you went outside, you had to watch Arcas get bigger and bigger in the sky as it came, and then smaller and smaller as it went away. At its closest distance, it looked about three times as big as the Moon.

Speaking of the Moon, as expected Arcas grabbed the Moon as it passed. Looking at a globe and calling the south end the "bottom" of the Earth, Arcas came "up" at us from the bottom. The Moon's orbit started wobbling when it began to feel Arcas's gravity. Its orbit around the Earth stretched into a larger elliptical shape until it swung around one final time and was handed off to Arcas. It's settling into an orbit there and gets to stay with Arcas from now on. You Arcasians will have it as a reminder of the old Earth. When you look up at the Moon, take some time to think about how your ancestors looked up at the same moon for thousands of years, but from a much different foundation underfoot.

Amidst the disasters and destruction Arcas brought, we had an unprecedented sight. We saw part of the dark side of the Moon from Earth. It's not an important event other than to note it's something we had never seen from Earth before. Nevertheless, it was a strange experience. It's nothing I had ever imagined being able to see before. Someone in our housing complex had a small telescope, and we took turns looking at the supply base on that side of the Moon. When it was my turn, I wiped my tired eyes and took a quick peek. It looked vaguely reminiscent of a shipping stockyard. Although the telescope wasn't very strong, I could make out rows of white containers. The crispness and color of the rows made it look a little like a circuit board. Looking at the Moon helped me forget briefly about the devastation happening in the world.

One of the first disasters caused by Arcas was flooding. The tidal pull of Arcas created an unprecedented high tide in the southern hemisphere. At the time, Arcas was still coming toward us along its straight line so the tides went higher on the Arcas facing side of the Earth and lower on the opposite side. The Moon and Arcas were on the same side of the Earth when Arcas was at its closest distance, and the tidal force of the Moon added to the effect as it orbited around the Earth and caused more chaos to the tides. It resulted in tidal surges that traveled over all of the lowlands. Then, as Arcas passed through our orbital plane, the highest tides shifted to the northern hemisphere. Anything lower than 250 feet elevation was submerged by tsunamis several times over the course of weeks.

The northern hemisphere had more time to prepare than the South. Thank goodness for tiny blessings, I guess. The Great Lakes sloshed back and forth in their basins. Chicago, Milwaukee, Cleveland, New York, Washington, Houston, New Orleans, Los Angeles, San Francisco, Hong Kong, London. They all had water surge through them repeatedly and are all but destroyed. Smaller buildings, cars, and other debris was pushed around by the flood waters. They collided into larger buildings each time the flooding went back and forth, and many of the larger buildings eventually fell when their bases were beaten and destroyed.

The whole state of Florida had waves of water flood over it from the east to the west. The Atlantic Ocean overflowed the Netherlands' seawalls. Those walls are holding the water in now; most of the country is completely under water. Like the flooding that crossed over Florida, the high tide sometimes ran over all the land in its path in other places and traveled around the world. Water from the Atlantic Ocean washed completely over Central America into the Pacific Ocean and kept going.

Every place near a fault line was affected by earthquakes. San Francisco had a double dose of disaster. They were flooded by tides first and devastated by earthquakes when their faults went off. Salt Lake City escaped the tidal floods because it's so high, but its fault went off in a big way. The valley floor dropped enough to cause water to flood into the Bonneville Basin again rather than draining out. The Great Salt Lake is filling to become a huge inland lake again.

Yellowstone erupted, too, but not to the extent you see in movies. The caldera blew up and spread ash eastward across the United States. There's a huge hole in the ground now with steam coming out. We're fortunate there wasn't lava blown out across several states.

Earthquakes, tsunamis, floods, volcanoes, avalanches. Whatever you can name, it happened. People died from collapsing buildings, enormous flooding, intense lightning storms, and other disasters. It was real Wrath of God kind of stuff. When the insurance companies say they aren't responsible for damage caused by an Act of God, this is what they're talking about. In my job, I've seen disasters, but rarely multiple at the same time.

More tragedy is following behind the disasters. So many people have died we aren't able to take care of their bodies. Many people are simply missing, too. We can't locate a lot of them and don't know if they're alive somewhere or if they're part of the casualties. It'll take time to gather the dead and make an accounting.

To compound the death from the disasters, there's been a second wave of suicides. I didn't mention it before, but there were quite a few immediately after the President first broke the news about Arcas. It settled down quickly, but picked up again after these disasters. People are depressed by having to face the reality of what's happening and are taking their own lives. The world governments are doing the best they can to clean up, but it's not going well. Meanwhile, bodies are decomposing wherever the people died which makes the job even harder.

Arcas is moving away, but the natural disasters are being followed by others. Wildfires have started all over, power lines are down (not that we had much power anyway), pipelines are broken, and communication lines are severed. Satellites are off course and going wild, too. Some look like shooting stars as they crash into the atmosphere, some are sailing out of their orbits, and the ones left aren't working well. And rioting has started again. The mobs are staying out during the day this time. I guess they don't see any reason to hide while it's light because there's nobody out to try to stop them. The military is too busy helping with all of the disasters.

On top of everything, as I mentioned earlier, our moon is gone. It's orbiting Arcas and is going away with it. Together they caused problems with tides when they were both here, but having the Moon missing is still causing tide problems. The problem now is the tides are smaller than we're used to. You wouldn't think having lower tides would be problematic, but the smaller ebb and flow process is causing problems.

Despite the destruction and death, there's a tiny ray of light in all of this. People are helping each other out. That is, the people who are left are helping. With all of the destruction, they're coming together for a single purpose: help thy neighbor.

As I said, Arcas is heading away from us now, but its straight line of movement is bending into a parabolic path as it gets closer to the Sun. Arcas and Earth are both moving in the same direction around the Sun, but the dance isn't over. As we go along our path around the Sun, Arcas will curve around the Sun and come back through our orbit. At that point, its interaction with Earth will change it to a circular orbit (i.e., one of Kepler's near circular ellipses) and tilt it into the same general plane as the other planets. With the swing that happens to Arcas, the Earth will be cast out of its orbit and will silently glide out of the solar system.

A saying of one of my grad school buddies comes to mind, "You've got to dance with the horse that brung ya." As ridiculous as it sounds, I always thought it meant: whatever your situation, you have to deal with it. I don't know. Earth is the horse that brought the human race this far in our civilization. We've danced with her for as long as possible, and now a new horse named Arcas is coming along. We've got a little less than six months to get ready to dance with a new horse.

41

JOURNAL
Ground Control to Major Tom

I miss professional baseball. The first pass of Arcas has decimated our "civilized" event schedule. Baseball isn't happening anymore. The teams still occasionally played before Arcas came, but there's nothing now. Before the power problems, I used to look forward to watching it on TV while drinking a beer or two. Max would make beer runs to the fridge for me when I needed a new one. He kept track of the game schedule and would get out bowls of chips and dip for us those nights. The housing complex has space for a small baseball diamond, and the kids have formed some teams to play. I think Jenny's mom has encouraged it as a physical education activity during the day.

Our plans for spaceships for the transfer to Arcas are coming along. Since Cape Canaveral in Florida was washed away by the tides, the launches will be tougher. We suspected flooding would happen when Arcas came by and made plans for floating launch pads. It's proven technology, thanks to the Briar Patch Group. The country has a flotilla of launching pads and ten times as many ships holding successive waves of rockets, and the next and the next. The flotilla will be sailed near the equator since it's the best place to launch from.

The billionaires of the world are doing the same thing. Even before Arcas came, a good amount of our industry had shut down. As construction of ships ramped up, people moved from other jobs to that sector. A lot of what I'd call nonessential manufacturing shut down. You know, we don't really need to make new picture frames or glow sticks at the moment. I think the workers from those sectors hope they have a better chance of winning a spot on a ship if they're working on them. It really helped to have all of the plans from the private space companies available. I just hope everyone followed them and didn't cut corners.

Other countries have been building spaceships, too. Not everyone who traditionally exported the materials we need are having open markets, so we've had to scramble for materials. The countries with the raw materials are hoarding them for their own ships. We've been recycling and reusing materials we already had in the country and have heard of some fighting at borders as countries are trying to get supplies.

Electricity and computer time is scarce, and a lot of it's been dedicated to calculating the trajectories of the ships. There's going to be so many of them, and we want to land them all in the same location. We've been sharing our landing zone with the other countries and the private sector hoping more people will land there. We'll see who wants to. A couple have agreed to try our spot, but some haven't given us any indication of where they're going. I grasp two sides of the situation; the human population is going to be so much smaller we're going to need every person we can get, while at the same time, having several separate groups of people will prevent the whole race from dying out if there's a bad disaster or other mortal danger.

Living on Arcas isn't going to be like living here. There won't be any infrastructure of any kind. Although there won't be any forest to clear, the colonists will have to build everything from the ground up. They'll easily be able to see the lay of the land for selecting sites. That's not to say it isn't going to be extremely difficult circumstances, though. Even starting farming is going to be a Herculean feat.

I just remembered something I wanted to write about. There's a rumor some greater millionaires and lesser billionaires have built biodomes to try to survive. I think they're creating huge underground structures to be air tight and self-sufficient. Huge is right. They'll have to have massive greenhouses for growing food and recycling carbon dioxide into oxygen. They'll need fully contained water and waste systems, and people to work them.

I don't know how they're going to have sustainable power without being able to go outside to get oil, refine it, and burn it. My guess is their best option would be to have their own nuclear reactors or some kind of geothermal generators. Both would last a long time, but geothermal would be less dangerous. The inside of the Earth will stay warm for thousands of years, if not longer, so they'll be able to stay warm after it passes out of the solar system.

Yikes, they must have people going through a similar process as we have to make plans. How exactly are they going to grow their food? How are they going to replace things when they break? I suppose they could go out in space suits to scavenge when they need something they don't have and can't make. The only air they'll have is what's in their dome. How are they going to know beforehand if it's completely air tight? If something goes wrong, the air will all be gone, and they'll be dead.

What are they thinking? What's their end game? Do they think the Earth will suddenly become habitable again? It took Arcas millions of years to come to us. The Earth'll be floating through empty space for millions of years before it gets near anything else. I find this rumor hard to believe. Still, it might be true. A drowning person will cling to anything floating nearby.

42
THE ASTRONAUTS
Supply Drops

Johnson and Peterson finished prepping for the next launch. Johnson sent a message to mission control with an update on their progress. It would take several minutes for them to receive it, a few more minutes before they received a confirmation, and an hour or more before Johnson and Peterson received a detailed reply with any adjustments to the launching and landing program for the next day. Johnson was happy when Beckson was at the CAPCOM desk because he had the most recent experience on the Moon and knew the most about the capsule arrangement. The communication delay had stretched from seconds when they were orbiting Earth to minutes after Arcas captured the Moon and began moving away. Johnson figured the delay would get shorter again after they pass around the Sun and head back toward the Earth.

Their mission would last longer than the other astronauts who had mustered the supplies on the Moon. They, along with Dobson and Richardson, were the transition team from the mission of stockpiling supplies on the Moon to dropping supplies onto Arcas. After sending the last canister, the four will be on the last launch from the Moon. They will be the final immigrants to the new world, and ironically the ones who had been off the Earth the longest.

Supplies were launched from the Moon every other day. On days without a launch, they loaded supply canisters onto one of the small rockets and prepped it for launch. With six months before the second Earth pass, they had to keep to a tight schedule, and it seemed like a grueling pace sometimes.

Six years' worth of accumulated supplies couldn't be dropped to Arcas in six months, but they had been given an aggressive timetable to ensure much of it would be waiting for the first people who landed. The canisters wouldn't be in neat stacks like they were on the Moon, though. They were being sent to one location, but were landing with parachutes. Depending upon the winds and entry locations, they'd be scattered across a wide area.

Each canister was numbered and the contents were itemized. Locating them would be like a vast Easter egg hunt with the colonizers searching to find each one. After recovering one, they might wonder where another would be. The numbering would help them know which ones were still waiting to be found, but they could practically pick any random direction to set off looking for them.

Johnson paused his work and looked up at the grey planet. He remembered how he watched Arcas while it came to Earth its first time. The Moon's rotation relative to its change in orbit made it possible for the astronauts to see the Earth at times, too. They experienced a few minor moonquakes as they witnessed the destruction happening on Earth, but didn't feel many other effects of Arcas themselves. Each peek they had of the Earth came with a new shock. They heard about the devastation in their communication messages, but were never fully prepared for the sight of it. Each time the Earth came into view, they saw a new snapshot of destruction. It crawled toward them visually in stunted steps that jumped from the beginning, to the middle, to the end without being able to see the full smooth transition happen.

They had watched in horror as the ocean waters flowed around the southern hemisphere and moved to the north to cross the Florida peninsula and Mexico. They saw the ash cloud from Yellowstone spread across the northern hemisphere and dissipate around the globe. They could see a portion of southern California move away to the west to create a water-filled gap between it and the rest of the United States. And finally, they felt a hollow sense of abandonment as they watched the Earth recede after the Moon started orbiting Arcas. It had affected all four astronauts, but Johnson felt it the most; he had been on the Moon the longest.

43

JOURNAL
Night and Day

The leaves are starting to turn in the mountains. I've always looked forward to the colors in Fall, partially because it means snow will follow for skiing. I don't know about this time, though. Something about watching the leaves die and fall off the trees for the last time reminds me too much I won't ever see them again. The Earth has less than six months to shift through seasons and life cycles. And that means Max has less than six months left to live. I feel bad for the children who won't be able to grow up and have a full life. It makes me deeply sad.

Now that it's passed, the computer modelers have finalized how Arcas will be rotating. They had a good estimate before, but solidified it. In its final orbit, it's going to be tilted by 88 degrees. That is, the North Pole is tipped 88 degrees relative to standing straight up on the north-south axis with the equator facing the Sun.

Maybe you know or maybe you don't, but Earth's tilt is slightly more than 23 degrees. The equator of our planet has sunlight coming from almost directly overhead year round, and has nearly equal periods of light and dark each day throughout the year. People living here on Earth range from near the North Pole across the equator to near the South Pole.

Living on the equator on Arcas will be much different than living on the equator on Earth. At one time of the year, the North Pole will face the Sun while at the opposite time of year, the South Pole will face it.

As I said, here the equator faces the Sun the whole year. It won't be that way on Arcas. At the North and South poles of Arcas, there'll be six months of constant sunlight throughout the year, and six months of darkness. The North and South poles will alternate between being frozen solid and thawing each year. Unlike the constant ice caps we have on our North and South poles, they'll be semi-annual ice caps and semi-annual deserts where the planet's magnetic field will funnel and collect solar particles. There's no way any colonists could survive there. Crops can't grow in those conditions so that's not where we're planning to start the colony. We're going closer to the equator.

Unlike a day at the equator on Earth, the days at the equator on Arcas will look much different. When the equator is facing the Sun twice a year, it'll be a hot summer, and there'll be day and night. When the poles are facing the Sun, the equator will have constant light, but it'll be very indirect. The farther you move from the equator, the more it'll be like the constant day/night cycles above the Arctic Circle on Earth. Because of this climate situation, we figure the best place for people at the beginning is at the equator. At least we know they won't freeze in desperately cold conditions or roast in interminably scorching sunlight. Maybe they'll spread to the north and south as they become more comfortable and adapted to the seasons.

Speaking of seasons, there'll be twice as many seasons throughout a year on Arcas. The closer you are to the equator, the more you'll experience two quick summers and two quick winters per year. The closer to the poles, the more it'll be one bright hot summer and one dark cold winter. In the right place near the equator, the winters will be chilly with a steady twilight while the summers will be hot with regular day and night. During the two summers per year, the crops will have a full day and full night to grow and rest. Farms will have constant light in the winters, but it'll be less intense. That's going to really mess with the cycles of the plants we're sending. Their yearly growing and dying back will need to speed up to twice as fast.

To help our colonists with the Arcas seasons and light, we've brought in consultants from Scandinavian countries. Their whole history and culture is used to having long dark periods during the year so they know a lot about it. They talk about how to be prepared for it psychologically and how to deal with it when the dark starts to bring you down mentally.

44

JOURNAL
Evolution at Work

For this journal entry, I don't want to write about what's going on now, but look ahead at the future. We've been wondering at work how plants and animals will change on Arcas. Higher gravity, fewer predators, less crowding, and different season cycles will result in quick evolution in the plants and animals. As they adjust to the new environment, Darwin's theory says advantageous adaptations will give organisms an edge that will win out over the ones that don't have them. Good mutations will win out rapidly. But, what will the winning mutations be?

My thoughts about the evolution on Arcas have coalesced into two ideas. Two ideas with three possible outcome combinations. Things will get bigger or things will get smaller, or maybe it could be some of both. Muscles, bones, and body structure could get bigger to handle the added strain of the higher gravity, or the size could get smaller to optimize energy use. I have no idea what will actually happen, but I'm thinking new species of plants and animals will emerge within just a few generations. People will start to change, too. We might become thicker or smaller. Either way, there'll be an evolution from Homo sapien into Homo arcasien. Would we even recognize people after a couple hundred years?

I wish I could be there to see it. What color will the wild flowers be? How tall will they grow? All the new species that'll develop might mean new structures and new systems. Evolution of the human population will take longer than I'd be alive to see, but the new species of plants and animals would be really interesting.

45
JOURNAL
Dilemmas

School would have started for Max by now, but there's no public school happening. We don't even know if there are enough teachers left to take students. Everyone who's available is working on the cleanup after Arcas went by. Even if we could find enough teachers, we'd have to find buildings for them to be in, and we'd have to protect them from anyone trying to scavenge food or other supplies. I'm happy that Jenny's mom is still leading the schooling in our compound. It keeps many of the adults occupied and gives the kids something to do. They have dances on some evenings that Jenny and I have gone to. It's nice to see the smiles on the kids' faces as they stand in a circle and cheer for their friends when they go to the middle and do some kind of dance moves. Young people's dancing is hilarious.

The colonist lottery has happened, and people have been selected for the transfer. The government waited this long so everyone would be motivated to stay involved with everyday life. They started notifying the additional people who were picked, but it isn't going as well as they'd hoped. Some people are turning it down. A larger number than you might suspect. Over fifty percent of them are parents who don't want to leave their families. Some of them are trying to pass their spot down to their children, but it doesn't work like that. An open spot goes to the next person on the list.

Other people are jumping at the chance to go. I understand their enthusiasm, but don't think they realize how difficult survival will be on Arcas. We're doing everything we can to make it habitable, but it won't be highly livable. They won't have the same modern-day luxuries or as much free time. Still, even with the difficult conditions, they'll have the luxury of living. A luxury the rest of us won't have.

I've thought about it, but can't say what I'd do if they told me I'd been picked. My team wasn't granted any special consideration in the lottery, so we have the same chance as everyone else. Everything in me would want to go, to stay alive longer. At the same time, it would be agony to be without Jenny and Max. It would feel like shirking my responsibility to take care of them. No, if it came to it, I think I would have to choose to stay on Earth and let someone else take my spot.

46

THREE QUEENS
Stephanie's Dilemma

Stephanie was surprised by the knock on the door. It was strange because nobody had knocked on the door in a long while. Steve wasn't there to answer it and send them away like he used to. If it was Steve coming home, he wouldn't have knocked. In fact, she hadn't seen or heard from Steve in months. She didn't know if he was alive or dead. It didn't really matter to her. She cared at first, but didn't anymore. He was never really around even when he was there, and life was better without him.

Without money from Steve, Stephanie and the kids had been hungry for a long time. They had all lost a lot of weight and were skinny. Stephanie was embarrassed to go outside because she could feel the neighbors stare at them. When she gave the kids a bath, she could see their ribs. Then one day, a bag of food appeared at her front door. She was uneasy about taking it at first, but was so hungry she gave in and took it inside after glancing around to see if anyone was watching. She was grateful the next week when another bag appeared. A new bag materialized every week from then on like a leprechaun's pot of gold, except this was better than gold; it was food.

Stephanie knew it must have been neighbors leaving the bag, but she never saw anyone come by. In appreciation, she tried to give a little smile when she saw people outside. It was hard to smile because she had spent so many years not smiling, but she forced the corners of her mouth up slightly as a way of thanking the anonymous donors.

When Stephanie answered the door there were two people in military uniforms standing outside. She stood inside with the door propped open a crack and her foot wedged against the back to hold it in place. It wouldn't stop them if they tried to force their way in, but she would put up a fight. Her face was near the opening so they could talk, but she didn't invite them in. Rather than push their way in, they asked politely if they could come inside. She told them no. She didn't want them to come in and see how she and her kids lived.

Her only thought was the army had come to arrest Steve for something he'd done. She told them Steve wasn't there and was surprised by the confused look on their faces. They assured her they didn't know who Steve was and gave her the shocking news she had been picked in the lottery to go to Arcas. The lottery was all people were talking about these days. Everyone wanted to be picked so they wouldn't die.

Stephanie didn't want to be picked, though. She was ready for an ending. Before they finished talking about the "wonderful opportunity" she was being given, she stopped them and told them she wouldn't be going. Her life had been hard enough, and she didn't want to prolong it. She had hoped for a quick death when Arcas passed the first time, but that hadn't happened. She closed the door and left them standing on the doorstep.

47

THREE QUEENS
Susan's Dilemma

Susan was surprised by the knock on the door. It was strange because nobody had knocked on the door in a long while. She and the neighborhood women got together often these days to help each other, but nobody bothered to knock during the daytime. They would make food for the group of families, work on laundry, and do other household chores. Each day they gathered at a different house to work on the chores. It began with two or three friends getting together for a few hours to be social and developed into a system of ten families on a rotation. There never seemed to be an end to the pile of socks with holes in the toes in need of mending and dishes in need of washing. They made the best of their time together every day and kept themselves cheerful.

The men in the families went out every day to do their best to work and provide for everyone. Their work situation was much different than it had been, but they were making the best of it. Some still had jobs and others didn't. They helped each other find work when they could and shared the odd jobs they found. Some days it was manual farm labor that paid with food, and others they helped with disaster cleanup. They protected each other when they were out and returned with whatever food, firewood, or supplies they found. It was important to them to take care of the families they were responsible for, and it was also important to them to take care of their friends in the neighborhood.

Susan stood on her tiptoes to peer out the small window in the top of the door and saw two men in military uniforms. She wondered what a coincidence it was they happened to show up at her house on a day the group was there. Most days there wouldn't have been anyone home to answer the door.

While she stood at the door, she said a quick prayer to herself before opening it, inviting them into the house, and suggesting they sit in the living room. As they sat, she offered them glasses of lemonade. She didn't tell them it was the last they had because it would have been rude. However, they knew there were severe food shortages and politely declined.

When they said her name had been picked in the Arcas lottery, Susan felt her face go flush. She thought for a brief moment before responding. She thanked the two men for coming by and told them to give her appreciation to their superiors. She was happy to have been selected, but had to turn them down. Her family was all she wanted, and she wouldn't leave them. She asked them to give her spot to the next name on the list. Thinking about being able to help someone else survive and get to Arcas gave her a big smile.

Susan stood and showed the gentlemen to the door. She thanked them again for their kindness in visiting, extended her appreciation to them for the service they were doing, closed the door behind them, and went back into the kitchen to continue folding clothes from the basket on the kitchen table. She didn't want them to feel bad she had been picked and they hadn't, so she made up a little white lie for the other women in the room about the soldiers asking for men who could help clear rubble from a building down the street. They may have heard some of the conversation from the other room, but didn't let on if they had.

Later that night, she mentioned the visit to Roger. He was upset at first when he heard she turned down the chance to go to Arcas. Like a good husband, he wanted the best for her, and the best outcome in these circumstances would be to go to Arcas. When she explained the loneliness she would feel on Arcas and the feeling of selfishness she would have after having gone without him and her children, he realized his mistaken viewpoint. Roger agreed he would have made the same decision and confessed sadly he hadn't thought about it in such real terms until then.

48
THREE QUEENS
Karen's Dilemma

Karen was surprised by the knock on the door. It was strange because nobody had knocked on the door in a long while. Dodger ran to the door barking his head off. They had been out earlier hiking on the mountain trails, and he was full of energy. It seemed like he had stopped to sniff every third bush along the way. They were both dusty, and Karen was tired. She needed to give Dodger a bath that night and wanted to go to bed early so she could get up to hike and see the sunrise in the morning.

When Karen opened the door, there were two men in army uniforms waiting. She bent over to hold Dodger's collar with one hand, held the door with the other, and cocked her head up to look at them. They wanted to come in to talk, but Karen didn't want any kind of military people in her apartment. She disliked the military because they killed Mother Earth's children and maimed Her land, so she declined. Instead, she stepped out while holding Dodger back with one open palmed hand signal and closed the door behind her.

One of the soldiers commented on how well-behaved her dog was, and how his little dog was always yipping when strangers came to the door. Karen thanked him curtly and asked why they had come. They told her she was chosen for the group to transfer to Arcas and had the opportunity to help colonize the new planet. Karen had no interest in being a part of that. She loved her Mother Earth, and there was no way she was going to leave Her. She declined, thanked them, and asked them to, "Please don't come by again," as she went back inside.

After that conversation, Karen decided to leave Dodger dusty for the night. She wanted to snuggle with him and smell the earth in his coat while she slept.

49

JOURNAL
A New Twist on Gravity

We were thrown a curve ball today. We get information at work before the general public, but the whole world will find out soon. It has to do with the gravity of Arcas and how close it's going to get. It's still not going to hit us, but it's going to get REALLY close.

When Arcas comes by in about four months, gravity is going to feel like it's going crazy when it's at its closest point. Because it has higher gravity than the Earth and because it'll be so close, they think its gravity is going to supersede the Earth's at times. None of this is anything we know for sure, though. They're using equations to predict what's going to happen in real life. I'm sure most of it's accurate, but it's hard to believe because we don't have any tangible experience to compare the theory to.

The first part of the news is Arcas is going to suction off some of our atmosphere. Heck, it's not like we'll be needing it anymore as we fly off into cold space. In a way, that's good news because it means there'll be more oxygen on Arcas along with other parts from our atmosphere, like ozone to block some of the Sun's rays.

The second part of the news was even stranger. It's possible things other than the atmosphere will be sucked up by Arcas, too. <u>Possible</u>. Water from the oceans could be sucked over to Arcas. Surface tension will keep the water formed into large blobs so it doesn't break apart into tiny droplets. And, they said, it could be possible for some things from the ground to be lifted into the air.

That last bit's going to get everyone thinking about how they can get over to Arcas on their own. Maybe they'll try jumping their car off a ramp at just the right moment and sailing over to Arcas. Or people with airplanes might try to fly high and hope they're taken over with the air.

Flying a plane or jumping a car won't work, of course. There's no way to survive through the empty space between the planets, but they won't think about that. There wouldn't be any way to land a car, either. You'd end up smashed like a crashed self-driving car. Hope always wins over practicality when things get desperate, though.

Although the scientists say things from the ground will be lifted up, they also say there won't be enough pull to get the more dense things to an escape velocity and past a tipping point. The tipping point is the point where something making it that far will either continue to Arcas or fall back to the Earth. Some atmosphere will get past the tipping point, some water will get past the tipping point, but none of the solid things really will. They just won't get the speed they need to make it.

Still, having things lift off the Earth gives me an idea. I have to think about it a little more. It's kind of harebrained, but I need to consider everything. After all, I'm desperate, too.

50
JOURNAL
Biodiversity

There are rumors some people are building contraptions to launch themselves from Earth to Arcas when it passes. They're word-of-mouth rumors because there aren't any news programs on television anymore. In fact, there isn't television anymore. On a good day, we barely have electricity for the lights and to cook with. There isn't enough to produce the nightly news.

The reliable news we get comes from the military. They're deployed around the country to help with rioting and disaster cleanup, and have a communication network set up.

I was thinking today how glad I am I don't have to leave the compound to get to work. Any crowds of people outside are likely to attack you to take any kind of property you have. I'm thankful that Jenny and Max don't have to go outside the compound's fence, either.

We've been stockpiling animals for Arcas, so to speak. The chicken weights have worked nicely so we outfitted other animals with weigh vests, too. We're placing a lot of trust in goats and sheep. Goats for their milk, although it tastes different than cow's milk, and both for their wool. Both also for a bit of meat and because they'll eat extra garbage plants and food (to start the composting process).

Since there haven't been any plants on Arcas, we'll be taking a huge seed bank aside from the seeds we've been sending for the terraforming effort. We have an idea of what will grow best, but want to send more for planting a second round after the first is established. It would be impossible to do this over the whole surface of a planet, but we have to get something started. There's going to be a lot of erosion and shifting of the dust over most of the planet. We can't have erosion where our people will be. It's imperative to get roots into the layer of Arcasian "soil" to hold it together. It would wipe us out if we couldn't anchor any plants to feed us.

The plan is to introduce as much plant-based biodiversity as possible. We're throwing a large plate of spaghetti squash at the wall to see what sticks. The plants will capture carbon from the air and convert it into biomass and organic compounds for composted fertilizer.

As far as animals go, we don't have the resources to transfer larger fish and animals to Arcas. The cost/benefit of sending elephants, or even cows, doesn't add up. We can send many times as many small animals in the space one elephant would take up, and they'll stand a better chance of survival in the higher gravity and harsh conditions. It pains me we have to decide which species will get a chance to survive and which will become extinct, but we have to make the hard choices to ensure the greatest chance of success.

We won't send elephants, but do we send turtles? Do we send raccoons? Armadillos? Even rats? We can get the animals there, but we also have to take sufficient food for them to survive until there are enough natural resources for them to live in the wild. These are tough decisions.

Back on the topic of seeds, human seeds are also going to Arcas. To provide for more genetic diversity in the future, we're going to send some frozen embryos. Even if you aren't picked to make the transfer trip, your genes can go to help you live on through the future generations. The labs supporting that effort will have priority for electricity.

In terms of the lottery, even though it's over, we had tossed around the idea of giving an advantage in the transfer lottery to pregnant women. If a woman is pregnant, that's two sets of DNA that would go to Arcas; hers and the baby's. The idea caused a lot of arguments amongst the team and higher up the chain. In the end, it didn't happen. How could we ethically make a policy to encourage women to get pregnant when a large number of them will be left on Earth to die? No, it didn't happen. However, it shifted to a policy discussion of encouraging the women who will be going to become pregnant beforehand. They'd get to make the decision themselves without being influenced by the lottery. I think some will and some won't. From my perspective, I hope more of them will.

51
EARTH
Rising Star (circa 8 years ago)

The facility was set back off a highway in New Mexico. It consisted of acres of computer servers in short buildings with one small office building and parking lot. There was no sign identifying it. The only signs on the razor wire fence surrounding the property said, "Keep Out," and, "No Trespassing." Each day fifteen men in dark suits drove through the guarded gate. Although this was the worldwide headquarters of an underground network, it didn't need more people. The group had members embedded in governments and businesses throughout the world, but keeping its numbers small in any particular location was one way it maintained its anonymity over a period of several centuries.

The system worked well. The organization was completely unknown to the public at best, and a rumor at worst. It was currently called Ancal, Inc. Nobody who suspected its existence had ever been able to prove it. Although some people tried, they never lived long enough to pass on their discovery.

The night before this particular sunny morning, the head of the organization, known informally in the office as Gianni, had sent out an appointment for a meeting first thing in the morning the next day.

Everyone who had received the email was gathered at the oval table in their conference room before the meeting start time. They chatted uneasily because none of them knew the reason for the abrupt meeting.

The honey colored stain of the wooden table shined in the light and helped brighten the room. It had been picked to reflect light and help illuminate the tapestry hanging on the wall. The tapestry, formerly a rug, was several hundred years old and had been passed down by members of the group as an heirloom from one generation to the next. Nobody knew the origin of the design. It was a representation of four horses pulling a Sun chariot. Even though the surface was worn, and the colors were faded from the years, it was revered by everyone at the table as a deep part of their culture and history.

Precisely at eight o'clock, Gianni walked into the room and strolled directly to the head of the table. He wore a luminous pink tie this morning. As he stood at the head of the table, it was difficult to tell whether the tie glowed from reflecting the lights in the room, or if it created its own radiance using some hidden power source.

"Good morning, gentlemen. And thank you for being prompt this morning." There were several chuckles from around the room as his joke broke the tension. In this organization, you weren't late for meetings, especially those called by Gianni.

"I'll get straight to the point. We've had a singular purpose for many generations. When our group was founded, its intent was twofold. First, keep the existence of the planet secret. Second, prepare the way for humankind's salvation. We've been very successful on the first front. On the second, we've had successes and failures, but have guided the world to a position where it's capable of travelling to the stars. As we've all known, our group's purpose will come to an end in our lifetime. It's time to prepare for the final stage.

"Before I go further, I want to reassure each of you; your dedication and determination to our mission has not gone unnoticed and will not go unrewarded. Each of you, and your families, will be incorporated into our plans to continue our work beyond Earth." He paused and slowly cast his eyes over each man sitting around the table to make sure the point was understood by every person in the room before continuing. "Now, on to the business at hand.

"Through our network, we've identified a young man at FEMA whose career is showing great promise. He's been recognized for his efforts and is developing into a disciplined leader. His name is David, or something. Or maybe that's his last name. I don't remember exactly at the moment, but it's in your briefing packets. We want him to be the leader of the culmination of our work."

Although each person seated at the table had a folder of papers in front of them, none had been opened. In this organization, you maintained focus on the meeting at hand, even when supplemental material was handed out. There would be plenty of time to read through the packet afterwards.

"We don't feel we need to alert him to our presence or the situation at this time, but will work him into a powerful level in his organization so he'll be ready to lead the charge. With us guiding his career, he'll be at the right level in FEMA when the time comes, not so high up he's ineffectual and not so low he isn't influential.

"Thanks to our passive data gathering network, we collect invaluable information on nearly everyone through their search engine queries, social media use, online purchases, voting choices, and more. We watch them on those front door cameras and listen to their conversations on their home assistant devices. I know I've said it before, but those doorbell cameras and in-home assistants were some of the most brilliant invention ideas we've profited from in a long time."

In truth, the group didn't only use technology for passive monitoring of the public. It manipulated global elections and corporate decisions subtly by affecting the social media feeds of their leaders. Before the social media era, they had an influence on the scripting process of radio and television programming. Their influence was pervasive and all-encompassing if you were in their sights. They even affected design and placement of billboard ads along certain commuting routes to alter subconscious choices.

Other groups were accredited, or blamed, for Ancal, Inc.'s actions depending upon the observer's ideology. Ancal, Inc. accepted the attributions, and did nothing to discourage the viewpoints or elucidate the misinformation. In fact, their network often encouraged the erroneous recognition in an active effort to remain anonymous.

"In addition to the aforementioned intelligence collection, we'll be assigning two members to begin an active investigation of his superiors at FEMA. If they don't naturally recognize and promote our new asset, we'll be able to convince them of his potential using the other means at our disposal. We can use our information to barter with them, and we're considering introducing one of our smaller pandemic candidates to have him seen working collaboratively with the Centers for Disease Control and Prevention's response team if enough other opportunities don't occur naturally.

"The next few years will be an exciting time for us all. It's been over 400 years since we started. In the beginning, the task in front of our founders may have seemed especially daunting to them. I'm sure there were times some of our members thought about giving up. Thanks to them, and thanks to you, I believe we've succeeded. Thank you for your help. Meeting adjourned.

"Oh, and one more thing," he said in an offhand tone as everyone stood up from the table, picked up their packets, and began to exit the room. "We're changing our name to Briar Patch Group. You know what to do. Carry on."

52

JOURNAL
Think a Happy Thought

The weather's steadily getting colder, but it isn't freezing yet. We're getting down to the 40s overnight and back up to the 70s during the day when it's sunny. I walked outside at lunchtime today to feel the sun on my face. I tried to get someone to go with me, but nobody was interested. The sun warmed up my shirt and made me feel toasty on my quick walk around the compound's outer fence. I had to carefully check each section as I made my way along the whole perimeter to make sure there wasn't anyone outside the fence. Even when you aren't outside the fence, having someone outside see you can make it a dangerous situation. You don't want to make a mistake and get caught daydreaming these days.

I started digging a hole today. I've thought about my harebrained idea for getting to Arcas and am going to try it. I've mentioned it to Jenny a couple of times. She's not on board, but I can't wait for her to come around. There's a lot of work to do, and it's dangerous to go outside the compound to do it, but none of us were picked in the lottery, and I'm feeling desperate.

Since gravity is going to be trying to pull things to Arcas when it passes, I've thought of a way we can try making the "gravity trip" ourselves. It's a huge risk, but the risk is worth taking compared to the alternative. There's a small-to-medium chance we'll live if we try it. There's a one hundred percent certainty we're going to die if we don't try.

We can't survive a "gravity trip" to Arcas without protection from the elements, or lack of elements as the case may be. The trip will take hours, if not days, and there's going to be very little air and atmospheric pressure, but we have an advantage other people don't. We have grandpa's bomb shelter. It's airtight, has its own air supply, and has a food supply. If we're inside when Arcas is at its closest and get pulled by the gravity, we could stay warm and breathe for the whole time.

That's not to say it'll be easy, though. There are lots of problems to work on. The foremost is the shelter is buried in the ground. Thus, I started digging a hole today. I need to unbury the shelter so Arcas can lift it up.

The basic plan is:

1. I free the shelter,
2. Arcas lifts it off the ground,
3. We give it a little propulsion push to get past the tipping point of falling back to Earth,
4. We stay warm and alive for as long as it takes, and
5. We parachute inside the thing to the surface.

It's simple, right? Yeah, simple.

The hardest part of starting was sneaking out of the compound. It's guarded to keep people from trying to come in which means it's hard for people to leave, too. I bribed one of the guards with extra food we had, and he gave me a "shopping list" to look for while I'm out. I'll have to spend some of my time foraging each time I'm out. Maybe it's better to describe it as scavenging than foraging. It's not the best situation, but it's what I'm going to have to do.

When I got to the old house to start working on this, it certainly didn't look the same. The neighbors were all moved out, and the mobs had come through. It was very beat up. Even more than what Max and I did to it. The front door was gone, and all of the windows were broken. Inside, the house was roughed up as I made my way past the garbage in the front hall. Luckily, they didn't burn houses as they went. The basement entrance to the shelter hadn't been found, but was blocked by debris. Thank goodness for small favors; the shelter was still intact.

Since the street's deserted, I'll be able to work without anyone noticing as long as I'm careful not to be followed or leave a trail on my way to the house. That's a real worry these days. The strong will take whatever they can from the weak so I have to be careful my own coming and going doesn't leave signs there's activity at the house. I don't have time to haul the dirt out of the yard and camouflage the hole each day, but the fence around our yard will help keep things hidden. I just have to hope nobody comes by and looks in the back yard.

53
JOURNAL
Dig the Whole Day Through

The shelter is unburied now. It took about two weeks of working in the evenings which didn't leave time to write in this journal. I had to work quickly because the weather will turn cold any time now. I didn't want to be trying to dig out frozen ground. As it was, we got a snow one night, but it melted as soon as it hit the ground.

I worked every evening for two weeks to dig out the shelter and stayed at the house a couple of nights rather than try to sneak back to the compound because it's too dangerous to be out at night. They were cold nights of sleep. About half of the time I stayed warm by working for a few hours after sunset. Thanks to the Moon being gone, I couldn't see well. There was starlight and light from the Milky Way to go by when it wasn't cloudy, but it only helped me not stumble into things as I walked back into the house. I followed the advice on how to eat an elephant: one spoonful at a time. One shovelful of dirt at a time. Fill two buckets and climb out of the hole to dump them. The piles didn't need to look pretty because they're hidden by the fence. Wearing extra weights for months was beneficial. I'm stronger than I used to be and have more endurance. Still, it was a relief when it was finished.

Step one of the plan is done: unbury the shelter. Step two will take care of itself: Arcas lifts it. The next piece of the puzzle is, well, a puzzler. We need propulsion to give us a boost once we're in the air. I'm not sure exactly how to do that. I can't just go out and buy rocket engines. Even if I could, there's no rocket fuel available; everything is being stockpiled for the ships being built. There are no spare rocket parts available for a budding, amateur backyard enthusiast such as myself.

The way I see it, the possibilities for propulsion are to expel gas from pressurized tanks or burn some type of non-rocket fuel I'm able to get ahold of. About the only thing I can discreetly search for without causing suspicion is propane. Natural gas might be better, but I can't find it in tanks. Rockets supply oxygen to burn their fuel, but we, fortunately, won't need to provide oxygen when we burn ours. There's going to be oxygen in the air until we get to a certain height. There might be a little beyond that, too, since our atmosphere is going to be stretching toward Arcas.

I'll get as much propane as I can scrounge in large canisters and hook up burners to it. I've seen enough pictures of rocket bell nozzles to try to fashion something similar. The fuel will burn, and the exhaust will be focused in one direction, toward the Earth, to push us in the other direction, toward Arcas. We can guide ourselves by watching the Earth through a security camera and turning the burner valves open and closed to make adjustments. Once the tanks are empty, we'll jettison them so we don't have that weight on the shelter. I'll have to lighten the shelter as much as practical in order to do this.

That sounds like a solution to step three, propulsion. Step four, staying alive during the transit, will also take care of itself. The shelter is prepared for that.

54

JOURNAL
Coming in for a Landing

The last step of our transit puzzle is landing the shelter without killing ourselves. When we get there, we'll be plummeting straight to the ground. Obviously, we need to make a parachute to slow our freefall. It needs to be bigger than it would on Earth because the gravity will be higher. To be safe, I'm going to over-design it. The parachutes will be bigger than the minimum I calculate as an extra precaution.

We'll also pack a bunch of air mattresses inside. Nobody wants those these days so I was able to find some in other houses easily. We can blow them up on the way over, and I hope they'll act like car airbags when the shelter lands and protect us from bouncing against the inside walls. With the size of the shelter, it's not going to be a gentle landing. I thought about rigging up some air mattresses to the outside that could be inflated if we had enough air supply, but have set the idea aside as too hard to engineer. We wouldn't have enough cushion thickness to do any good, and the material isn't the ultra-strong stuff NASA uses when it bounces landers on Mars, so it would burst. We'll have to rely on being cushioned on the inside during the landing. With the mattresses inflated, we'll be wrapped up like puffy burritos. Mostly lots of puffy shells with us substituting as the delicious burrito insides.

The parachutes aren't going to be anything special, but I hope they'll do the trick. Instead of one parachute, I'm going to make six. The lunar capsules NASA used had a set of three parachutes. I assume it was for redundancy in case one of them had a problem. By the same token, I don't want us to be reliant on a single parachute and have it fail. I'm going to attach a set of three parachutes at each end of the shelter. The shelter's a long cylinder so we'll try to balance the fall of each end. Two sets of three will make six parachutes. Preppers have a saying, "Two is one, and one is none." If any fail, there'll be back-ups. Still, it's going to be a bumpy landing to say the least.

55
JOURNAL
Spaceship Jenny

The parachutes are done. It took time to gather enough fabric and cut and sew it. Jenny and her mom worked on them during the day when they had time. I'm grateful to them because they were able to get them finished much quicker than if I was doing it.

I'm happy the shelter is finally ready. In theory, that is. The parachutes are packed and set up with a simple trigger we can activate from inside with a switch. The air supply and food stores are full. The air mattresses and cushions are in place. I even packed my scuba gear so I can dive on Arcas, assuming we make it. Maybe I can use it to dive for a supply capsule if we locate any underwater. Listen to me being positive about our chances of survival. My hope is still alive.

And, of course, I'm going to pack this journal. There'd be no use in writing down my thoughts over the past two years only to have them stay on Earth. I've done what I can to the shelter as far as planning and building. The rest is up to the laws of physics and an abundance of prayer.

I've christened the shelter to be Spaceship Jenny. Why, you ask? Well, because I made it, and I get to name it. I thought about naming it after myself, the Gene Machine, but using a man's name is bad luck. Anyway, I painted the name on the outside and christened it. We didn't have a bottle of champagne to smash against it, so I smeared dirt on it instead. I thought it would be nice to wish it well with a piece of the Earth.

56
JOURNAL
Time's Up

It's time to send people to Arcas. I haven't been able to sleep well for the past month worrying about our preparations. The questions have been on my mind constantly. Have we thought of everything? What haven't we thought of? Are we giving the colonists the best possible chance? Could we have sent more supplies and materials? I have the same thoughts about Spaceship Jenny and my own plans. I can share my concerns about the large-scale plans at work, but can't talk to anybody about Spaceship Jenny. Out of necessity I've kept it a complete secret. It would be too dangerous for us if anybody else knew.

Arcas is back, although it's not quite all the way here. It looks about as big as the Moon right now. Well, as big as the Moon was before Arcas took it away, that is. I held my thumb up to the sky and thought about how the Moon used to be half the size of my thumbnail. It's hard to remember what the Moon looked like, except we see it as a smaller bright spot orbiting Arcas as it gets nearer.

Before Arcas gets much closer, we're starting the transfers. At its closest, it's going to be about six to seven times as big as the Moon used to be in the sky. With launching rockets from floating platforms, we can't wait until Arcas is at its nearest point. We have to do the launches before the ocean tides start to get too wild.

Next week we're going to start sending the first rockets. They have completely automated guidance and landing systems. To conserve life support resources, we're inducing comas on everyone and will be fitting them with IVs to keep them fed, and fitting with other tubes for waste. The trip is going to take a few weeks, and space in the rockets is really limited, so we have to pack people tightly. With everyone unconscious, they won't get stir-crazy not being able to move around. They won't breathe as much air, either, so we were able to save some load that way. For some of them, it's more complicated because they're pregnant. About one in ten women decided to get pregnant before going.

It won't be the most glamorous trip, but they'll make it and keep humanity going. The ship systems will automatically wake them after they land. In addition to saving space, food, and air, they'll be more relaxed for the landing, which we expect will help prevent injuries. Ideally, the capsules will be upright when they land, but we've prepared them for the possibility of being capsized and more disoriented when the settlers wake up. Regardless, they'll have one heck of a headache.

We've let other countries know our landing area in case they want to join our colony. Our supplies have been going to the site for a while, and we've been laying down layers of plant seed as widely around it as we can. It may be a little spotty because we're trying to drop spreads of seeds and fertilizer on a small area from far away, but we hope some of it will overlap and grow. I personally added some chickpea seeds to the mix so people could make falafel.

I don't know if the people are completely ready, but who knows if they'd ever be? In the last few weeks, some of the former moon astronauts came and talked to them. I think it was mostly to calm their nerves by comparing what their experience will be with stories about more extreme space travel. The colonists have all of the training we can give them, and they've moved out to the staging areas. I wish them godspeed on their trips.

57
JOURNAL
Safe at Home Plate

We had good news today. The first of the colonist capsules have landed on Arcas! Since our TV, radio, and internet systems aren't working, it's hard to say how many people around the world will hear the news, but I hope some do. It's jumping around the country between groups of military via their radio system, and they've spread it to communities from there. What a relief! I feel like my perpetual headache may start going away.

There aren't a lot of working large telescopes, but the ones available watched the capsules as they made their trip. They were able to see some of the landings, and the capsules themselves automatically signaled their landing information. After landing, the colonists woke up and also made contact with Earth. They've had a hard time in the increased gravity, but we knew we couldn't perfectly replicate those conditions here and tried to prepare them mentally for that. They're managing as best they can. Having the gravity pull evenly at your whole body is different than wearing a weight vest. I imagine your hair will lay flatter there, too, but a bad hair day is the least of their worries right now. They'll adjust after a few weeks of constant exposure to Arcas's gravity.

The colonists have set up their first shelters, planted a flag, and located a few of the supply capsules from the Moon. They'll be busy looking for newly arriving colonists and previously dropped supply capsules every day, but I hope they don't forget the activity timeline from training: first things first. The total population of humanity on Arcas is no more than a few thousand. It's very fragile and any mistake could cause our whole race to go extinct. They have to ensure their basic survival needs, find a safe place to live, find a place to store supplies, and work on planting crops.

In the past, the Briar Patch Group has been the first to give us information about Arcas and what's happening. For example, they told us the orbit and tilt before we heard from other sources. Their suits and ties have been conspicuously absent for weeks, though. They must've had their own plans and skedaddled when we started sending colonists. I guess I can't blame them. They did their job to get things prepared and didn't need to exert their influence further once the capsules were sent. I wonder if their capsules are painted black with a bright tie symbol. Hmmm. I also wonder if they're going to the same location or if they've picked somewhere different for some reason.

The news we got wasn't all good, though. It's being kept quiet because I don't think the government wants people to hear bad news right now, but a few of the capsules didn't make it. There's enough chaos and depression around the world at the moment without throwing gasoline on the fire.

We heard the news when a special visitor from the army came and briefed us. He swore us to secrecy, yet again. The capsules he told us about made it to Arcas, but they didn't touch down successfully. Almost everything worked, but their guidance was off or it may have been too windy. Some capsules were off course and made corrections during their descent to come down on land, but ones that were too far off course couldn't. They landed in the ocean area.

Like all the colonists, the ones in the off course capsules hadn't woken up yet when their capsules landed. There was no escape for them, and they sank in their cells within the capsules. I try not to think about that, though. Unfortunately, it isn't like they died without knowing. The capsules were airtight for space travel. They wouldn't have flooded and drowned the people in their sleep. After coming down, the computers would have started waking the people up. They would have awoken inside the capsule, possibly tipped on its side, with no escape. Depending upon the depth, it may have been dark outside the windows. Whether or not they realized where they were, at some point they would have figured out they couldn't open the door due to the pressure of the water outside. I can't think about what it would be like to be trapped in that small space with little food and water while the oxygen and power slowly faded away.

I'm sure the people on Arcas know about the errant capsules and hope they'll memorialize them.

To whomever may be reading this journal in the future, I apologize for the upsetting turn toward the end of the entry above. It started positive and became darker as I thought about the colonists who didn't make it. I'd met each of them at some point during their training.

We tried to the best of our abilities to set the program up for success. We truly did. It was great news when the colonists made it, but was devastating to learn some didn't. I can honestly tell you the conference room was deathly quiet when they told us about it. We all felt personally responsible for those deaths.

I've tried to keep this journal accurately with my thoughts and observations about what's happened without including too many details describing the gruesomeness that arose in the world throughout the past couple of years. There were riots and disasters and panics, but watching how terrible situations are and how cruel people can be to each other was enough for me. I didn't want to relive it in my mind in order to write it down.

58
JOURNAL
Settling Down

Since colonists have been landing on Arcas, my team's job is close to being done. Arcas is getting closer, and the time is coming for my Spaceship Jenny plans. Jenny, her parents, Max, and I will have to "disappear" from the living compound soon. I'm not sure how much longer the army will continue to protect it anyway. They might pull out and leave us civilians to ourselves. We need to be at the shelter and ready when our time comes.

There's been additional news from the colonists on Arcas. As expected, their first days have been very hard. Not only are they affected by the gravity to a greater extent than we could prepare them for and need more food because of it, but they're physically drained from the different atmosphere. It's an exhausting place. It has oxygen for them to breathe, yes, but doesn't have the same balance of gases as on Earth. Our bodies have evolved to work in the conditions we have here. There are different amounts of gases in their air. Even the atmospheric pressure is different. The human body can adjust to different conditions as long as they're within a certain range. I sincerely hope they are.

The telescopes watched a storm sweep through the settlement last week. It blew dust over them followed by some rain. Although not an ideal situation, the colonists weathered the storm in the first of the domes they're building. The fact there was rain is a good sign for being able to grow crops. Let's hope future storms aren't more severe and cover the crops in dust.

59
EARTH
Bon Voyage

Gene, Jenny, her parents, and Max stole out of the housing compound and moved into the shelter ten days before Arcas would be at its closest point. He knew the rest of the team would wonder where they were, but hoped they wouldn't look for them; their work was done. The second round of natural disasters caused by Arcas's gravity had started weeks before and was more intense as Arcas was closer to the Earth. The small family wasn't sure when things would start to be lifted by Arcas's gravity and didn't want to miss the opportunity when it came. The shelter was ready to go with or without them. They wanted it to be with them.

It had been nine uneventful days, aside from the snow they'd gotten nightly. Uneventful in the sense the shelter was boring, but the rest of the world was undergoing major events. The transfer ships had all landed on Arcas. The gravity tug from Arcas was moving the tides more than it had the first time, and people were panicking. More people were dying from disasters, and more people were killing themselves out of desperation.

It was 4:08 a.m. when the shelter starting to rock back and forth. At any other time, they might have thought it was an earthquake shaking the shelter. The shelter had briefly trembled now and then during the previous days from huge earthquakes on distant faults, but this time the shaking felt continuous and determined. It was time. Arcas was starting to take some of the atmosphere from the Earth. Ocean water and other objects would follow soon.

They woke up and gathered in the middle of the shelter to be together. Gene checked the controls for the thruster burners again, something he had done compulsively for days. He knew they were ready, but he couldn't help himself. It took his mind off the intensity of what was going to be happening.

Functioning in the shelter was difficult because the gravity pull was also affecting the occupants. Their stomachs felt queasy, like they were full of butterflies, as they became more weightless. They were feeling lighter and could jump and bounce around the shelter. They laughed nervously as they leapt here and there to prepare some food to calm their nerves. They weren't sure whether or not they were supposed to enjoy the experience.

After an hour or two, the shelter stopped rocking and started to sway more gently and steadily. They could tell it was lifting up, but something didn't feel quite right. They were moving and swaying, but it seemed like loose items inside the shelter were rising toward the ceiling. Everything, including the shelter, should have been pulled toward Arcas at the same rate.

Suddenly, Gene realized what was happening. *Something's preventing us from being lifted up. The shelter must be tethered to the ground,* he thought. *What are we going to do?* His stomach sank as he realized the answer before finishing his thought. Someone was going to have to go outside to detach whatever was holding them down.

Gene took Jenny to one end of the shelter and told her what was happening and what had to be done. She didn't like the idea of someone going outside because she didn't know if they'd be able to make it back inside the shelter. He assured her he'd come back inside as soon as he loosened the shelter from what was holding it down. He lied and said there were plenty of rough hand holds on the outside.

Gene grabbed his scuba gear and headed for the shelter door. He didn't know what the conditions would be outside. Objects could be floating in the air, there could be water surrounding them, or the air could be thinner and hard to breathe. He didn't want to take chances with not being able to do the work that needed to be done by not having enough air.

Jenny's parents quickly discerned the situation, and the group began arguing about who would go outside. Eventually, Gene put his foot down and told them he was the only one who knew both the shelter and where tools would be to do the job. He was going.

Gene pulled on his wetsuit for protection and to stay warm. He put on his air tanks, told Jenny and Max he loved them, told them to be brave, went out the door, and latched it behind him. They'd be able to see him with the cameras installed outside.

Once he was outside, Gene immediately felt the upward tug of Arcas and had to grab onto the door's handle to keep from floating away. There was enough pre-dawn light to see, and the air around him was cloudy with snow and loose dirt that had risen from the yard. He looked up at Arcas and saw how large it was; much larger than ten days ago. It was bright in the pre-dawn light and took up a big portion of the sky. It was a few thousand kilometers away at this point, but would get closer. Although he couldn't see it, the atmosphere of the Earth was being stretched and drawn toward Arcas. *That's a big planet,* was all Gene could think before turning his attention to the task at hand.

He had to hold onto the outside of the shelter to pull himself around to the bottom and see what was happening there. When he got there, he saw a chain linked from the shelter to a concrete footer in the ground. *At least it's only one chain*, he thought. He worked his way into the narrow space underneath to check the chain and found a quick link at the top, the kind that had a screw on one side so it could open and let a chain link pass through it. He looped his legs around the chain to steady himself and started unscrewing the link to get it open. It wasn't an easy task to unscrew a quick link manufactured in the 1940s that had been buried in the ground for decades. Gene was glad, once more, he had kept wearing weights because he had more strength to work.

When the quick link was open far enough to pass the adjacent link through, Gene hooked his fingers through the links and pulled the chain to get some slack in it. It wasn't easy pulling the large mass of the shelter against Arcas's tug, but he managed to move it the few inches he needed and slipped the link through the quick link. As soon as it was loose, he spun around quickly, gathered his legs under him as best he could in the tight space, braced his back against the bottom of the shelter, and pushed off the ground as hard as he could giving the shelter a resolute shove with his arms. He knew he didn't have enough grip on the shelter to get back inside and wanted to get it moving as fast as he could so his family would have the best chance possible. As it moved away, he floated after it at a slower rate.

The shelter drifted away from Gene as he tumbled slowly in the air. *Jenny or her parents must know what's going on. They need to start the burners to start building speed.* For what seemed like an eternity, the shelter glided away slowly. *Get out of here! Get moving before the chance goes away!* Gene screamed in his head. It wouldn't have done any good to try yelling at them because they wouldn't be able to hear it. Gene kept giving them the "okay" and heart signals with his hands and waved at them to go in case they could see him. Each time the shelter came back into his vision as he spun, he wound up his body and gave a thrashing wave with his arms that would start him turning in a slightly different direction. Eventually, he saw the burner jets glow as they started up, and his eyes filled with tears of joy. He let out a relieved laugh and waved a final goodbye to Spaceship Jenny. *They did it.* The jets flared a little now and then as his family inside guided the shelter. After that, Gene calmed his mind and settled in to drift and watch the shelter for as long as he could before his eventual deadly drop back to Earth. He knew he wouldn't survive, but Jenny and Max would. He was sure of that in his heart.

Gene continued to drift upward for a couple of hours. Around him, he could see debris lifted from the ground rising and falling slowly as it went. He lost sight of the shelter after an hour and a half when he turned back after one of his slow tumbles. *What a beautiful sunrise,* he thought despite the spottiness of other material in the air. From his high vantage point, the sun shown with a new warmth as it crested over the expansive horizon. An initial deep purple color transformed into layers of reds, oranges, and yellows that stretched broadly across the sky as the sun made its way up. *I'm glad my last one looked like this.* He drifted and tumbled.

On one of the circles, a strange site caught his eye. It looked like a cloud, but was translucent and slightly reflective. The only thing that registered in his mind was it looked like a large amoeba moving through the air. It was huge and undulated slowly like a three-dimensional accordion. There were similar blobs farther past it.

As he watched it come toward him, he realized the blobs were huge balls of water. Something inside the closest one seemed to be moving. *That looks like a whale*, he thought. *This must be water from the ocean.* There were smaller fish swimming, too, and he could make out a pod of dolphins trying their best to stay together. The whale, however, was having trouble. It flapped its body back and forth as it tried to keep itself righted in one orientation. Nothing in the whale's life had prepared it for the situation it was in.

As the water blob came closer, Gene could see it was going to collide with him and envelope him when they met. As it happened, he put his respirator in his mouth, gasped at the sudden shock of the cold water, and prepared to take a ride. Although he was in the water, he was still tumbling, Gene stayed still to conserve his air supply. He could tell the water was picking up speed because the Earth was receding away very quickly. *This blob of water is going to make the trip*, he thought, *and I'm in it! I'll be making the trip, too, if I can survive the time.*

As he looked past the edge of the water, Gene could see other blobs of water moving from Earth to Arcas. He couldn't see blobs of air, but knew they would be going, too. He saw other solid objects, but they were far behind. He knew they would eventually go crashing back to Earth after Arcas was past.

Although he couldn't make out the exact edge of the water, the view through it was becoming more translucent. The outside edges of the water were solidifying and freezing. The whole mass was locking into a natural capsule as it continued to travel between the planets. The layer of ice on the outside prevented water from evaporating into space and acted as an insulator so the water inside didn't freeze solid.

Gene was so cold in the water he could barely stay awake. His whole body shivered in waves. The shivering started, built in intensity, and stopped after a sudden, last shudder. After a few seconds, the shivering would start again. Gene hugged his arms across his body to preserve as much heat as possible. His hands and feet felt like ice, and he couldn't move his fingers or toes. He passed out and drifted.

60

ARCAS
Bonjour

Gene awoke in the dark to the sound of a soft hum. It was a monotone note that paused and repeated itself in slow succession. As the fog in his mind cleared, he realized the hum was moaning coming from himself with each breath. His whole body was cold, and it hurt to try to move. When his foggy mind cleared enough to open his eyes, everything was blurry. He raised a hand to his eyes to rub the blurriness out with a knuckle, but stopped when it bumped into the plexiglass of his mask. *That's right*, he slowly thought, *I'm still floating in this water*. After blinking several times he could see Arcas looming large ahead of him. His mind was still too numb to feel how cold he really was. The coldness of the water had acted to slow his metabolism and keep him alive.

He thought he could see a hint of green here and there as he got closer to Arcas, as if there were patches of plants growing. Gene already knew their terraforming plans had been successful on a partial scale, but started to congratulate himself and everyone on his team anyway on the culmination of a successful plan for seeding a planet. He stopped when he realized he was speeding up. Panicked thoughts replaced his relieved thoughts. *I don't have a parachute and this water is going to smash to the ground*, he thought. *I'm not going to make it.*

Blobs of water were crashing to the surface of Arcas. Gene's blob crashed on the side of a small mountain. The heat of entering the atmosphere had melted and broken apart the ice shell. Gene tumbled over and over as the water came down. At the beginning of his wild ride, he brushed over the top of the whale as it tumbled past. He was beaten and bashed against rocks as the water carried him to the lowest elevation it could find and settled there.

When the wild ride finished, Gene shook his head to clear it. His heart was pounding and his body ached. *I'm alive! The water cushioned my fall. Ow! My arm feels like it's broken. Where am I? How do I get out of here? Which way were the green patches?*

He bobbed up to the surface of the water and swam toward what looked like a shore. His arm was useless so he lay on his back with it crossed over his chest and kicked through the water. The exertion of swimming with a broken arm was incredible as each leg kick caused his upper body to tense in a counter move that wiggled his arm. Every few minutes he stopped to float and let the pain subside. He floated and watched other blobs of water crash in the distance with enormous force. *How did I survive that?* was all he could think each time one struck the ground.

When he had swum to shore, he slowly dragged himself out of the water and lay on the rough ground, his arm throbbing. The shore was rocky without any dirt or plant life. He didn't know where he was or where anyone else had landed, but he had an idea which direction the green patches were. That was the direction of life. Since he had survived and the shelter had been farther ahead of him, he was sure it had also made it to Arcas. He silently prayed it parachuted safely.

After laying on the ground for many minutes, Gene pushed and grunted his way up to his feet. Coughing with each labored breath in the different atmosphere, his heart pounded in his ears as it pumped harder to push the blood around his body in the heavier gravity, and his broken arm burned as it was pulled toward the ground. He painfully worked his way out of his gear, dropped the tank on the rocks soundly with a metallic thud, picked a direction, and set off to find his family.

THE END

EPILOGUE

In the time after the Earth left its orbit, it snowed as the temperature grew colder each day. Winter had begun in the northern hemisphere before Arcas's second pass, but it was now winter everywhere around the world and many places were completely frozen. The snow stopped eventually as less water could evaporate into the air to create clouds and snow.

The air was very dry, and anybody who had the energy to go outside carried a water bottle. Every exhaled breath became a brief white cloud before it quickly dispersed. People who exerted themselves too long without drinking water were in danger of becoming light-headed from dehydration, collapsing, and dying.

The Earth had become a bleak tomb occupied by corpses in winter coats. People went outside only long enough to find food or something to burn to stay warm. The only animals left were those strong enough to protect a water source from intruders, and they didn't stray far from it.

Food had been scarce for Stephanie and her kids in the months after Arcas ejected the Earth from its orbit. The climate grew colder each day, and people stopped trying to grow food. The weekly bag of food had continued to show up on her doorstep, but it gradually held less. *Whomever has been leaving food for us must be hurting for food themselves*, Stephanie thought to herself. *I hope they haven't been suffering for us. We're not worth it.*

The kids were emaciated. They cried often because they were hungry and cold, but Stephanie couldn't do anything about that. They were lying in bed together as the room grew colder and colder. Being smaller, the children stopped shivering first, gently fell asleep and died in Stephanie's arms. Steve had not been home since long before Arcas's second pass. They were alone as the world grew colder. As she continued to cuddle with her children and hum to them, Stephanie succumbed to the cold herself. They all laid in the single bed, wrapped in blankets. The deep cold settled in further and froze one last tear on Stephanie's cheek.

Susan died bundled in her winter coat with her family and friends in their living room. The last days with her family had been precious to her. She loved them so much. They were a family and had stayed together until the very end. She was glad she made the effort a couple of days before to go down the block and visit with the woman who lives there. Susan didn't know her, but knew she had a very trying life. She and Roger had been leaving a portion of their food for her and her little ones each week. It had made their lives harder, but had brought them happiness to finally be helping this woman.

They kept a fire in the fireplace for as long as they could for the small amount of heat and light it provided. Susan died as the flickering light of the small fire danced on her cheeks. As Roger felt himself getting colder, he was barely able to keep his tired eyes open. He looked down at Susan in his arms one last time, slowly lifted his hand to gently wipe a tear from her face, kissed the top of her head, and went to sleep.

Karen's lifeless body sat on the top of Mount Hope. She had known it was time to go there when Mother Earth told her. She and Dodger packed plenty of water and made the laborious hike to the top in the cold, thin air for the last time. On their way, they had met a pleasant woman in a winter coat with a large fur-lined hood coming out of an apartment building. She cautiously stopped to say a melancholy hello and gave Dodger some smooches. She was going home to start making some food with her family and friends, and kindly invited Karen to join them if she could. After Karen thanked her and politely declined, the woman wished them a blessed day as she continued home.

Karen had noted over the past few months the Sun was growing dimmer and more distant. Bodies of water froze that had never frozen before. She felt each day in her soul as they ticked past and the weather turned colder, and went out often to recharge her spirit in the beauty of her Mother's creation.

Karen and Dodger were the only living creatures who climbed Mount Hope these days. The snow on the path was compacted by their frequent trips. There hadn't been fresh snow to forge a path through in a long time. At the summit of Mount Hope, she sat down in her usual area cleared of snow to watch one last dimming sunrise. She thanked her Mother for Her gifts and for her life. As she died, a tear rolled from her eye and froze at the top of her slender cheekbone.

Dodger sensed something had changed in Karen. He walked over to where she was and curled up into a ball next to her. He knew his place was at her side. After all, he was all she had.